MY WAY BACK TO YOU

NEW YORK TIMES BESTSELLING AUTHOR

CLAIRE CONTRERAS

MY
WAY
BACK
TO YOU

The hardest part is coming to the realization that no one is really going to save you but yourself, that pain is your life's most valuable teacher and that you will never find happiness until you are completely in love with yourself. That's all.

R.M. DRAKE

CHAPTER ONE

TESSA

I PULLED my trench coat shut and crossed my arms over myself in hopes that it would shield me against the cold wind as I neared the hotel. One of the perks of working for Prim was the conferences they sent me to. In the last seven months, I'd visited Spain, Milano, Venice, Rome, Cannes, and London. More places than I'd been to in my life before this, for sure. Every trip brought new information, new experiences, and I was gladly taking it all in. I hadn't been designing as much as I thought I would, but I'd been learning more than I thought imaginable in such a short period of time. My boss, Yamina, said she was trying to groom me for success. Prim would open their U.S. branch soon, and they'd be looking for people to head the departments, which meant I had a real shot at big-time growth in the company. The idea both terrified and elated me.

The bellhop greeted me with a smile as I walked inside. "Good morning, ma'am. Are you arriving for the conference?"

"Good morning, yes, would you mind pointing me in the right direction?" I smiled as wide as my stingingly cold face allowed me.

"Take the corridor to the left. You'll see the registration tables there."

I'd been there seven months and my French was still pretty awful. They just spoke so fast and had this thing they did with the back of their throat when they pronounced words. It was lovely to listen to and difficult to imitate. I'd spent hours in the café by my apartment just listening to people around me talk. Thankfully, most people understood English and spoke it better than I could imagine myself speaking French. Much to my chagrin, my sister seemed to have no problem picking it up. Though, I had a slight suspicion it had something to do with an elusive man she'd met a few months ago. She'd broken up with Ben and started dating the new guy shortly after she moved to Paris to be closer to me.

My phone vibrated in my pocket just as the woman at the registration table handed me my badge. I fished it out quickly and smiled at the sight of Cody's name on the screen. Cody, the buyer from Barney's I'd befriended and stayed in touch with, frequented these conferences as much as I did. The fashion industry was a small world and coming to these conferences made you see that. I answered the call before it was sent to voicemail.

"Where are you?"

"I just walked in." I pushed forward through the crowd that had gathered around the tea and coffee table. "This place is a madhouse."

"I told you."

"Yeah, but I didn't believe you."

He chuckled into the phone. "I see you. At three o'clock."

My eyes bounced to that direction. He was wearing a powder-blue suit that matched his eyes, and his blond hair brushed neatly to the side. I smiled, disconnected the call, and slid my phone back into my pocket as I reached him.

"Look at you, vest and everything." I reached up to kiss him on both cheeks.

"Look at you embracing the European culture."

I laughed. "You too? Samson gave me a lot of crap about it last time he was here."

"Sam is the brother of you-know-who?"

"Yes." I smiled because he remembered not to mention Rowan's name.

"How's he doing these days? Last time we spoke, you said he was going in for an MRI."

I swallowed thickly, trying to contain the emotion brought on by those simple questions, but a stupid tear broke rank and slipped down my cheek. Quickly, I wiped it away and then cleared my throat. "They found a mass in his brain and did a biopsy to confirm that it's cancerous. He's staying positive and says he's fine, but I feel like I need to see him in person to determine that for myself. He will be in town this week to see a doctor here."

Sam had said it was nothing serious, as if that diagnosis were ever a joke, but he was dealing with it as best he could, and if that meant making light of things, then I'd follow his lead. He'd be staying with me for a few days while he saw the specialist. Apparently, the research in Europe was more advanced than what we had back home.

"You're a good friend." Cody put a hand on my shoulder and stood in front of me to look me in the eye. I smiled shakily. "Let's talk about something else. I wouldn't want you to ruin the tough reputation you've built in the industry in such a short amount of time."

"You're right." I cracked a smile. "Do you think anyone noticed?"

"I think you're safe." He grinned before placing his hand on my expansive belly. "Any names yet?"

"Nope."

"You aren't going to be one of those hippy moms who waits to name her baby until after she takes it home, are you?"

I swatted his hand away playfully. "It's a baby not an it, and no." I laughed before hooking my arm around his and letting him lead me into the first room. "I just can't think of any names. I feel like I need to look him in the eyes first."

"Hippy mom."

"Says the guy wearing the powder-blue suit."

"I'm a trend-setter, darling."

We got a few dirty looks as we walked into the room for being loud, which made us cling to each other tighter as we fought to stifle our laughter. We moved to the front of the room quickly, found two seats in the second row, and got comfortable.

"This is more crowded than Milan," Cody whispered.

"It's because this is the hi-tech one," I whispered back. "They're going to show us whatever groundbreaking technology they're using to put the material together."

"I'm only here because it's mandatory. I've already been to three of these presentations." Cody pulled back and looked at me, eyebrows pulled up. "So, what are they teaching you at Prim?"

I laughed. "You ask me this every time we see each other."

"And you never answer my question."

"Because you're making me think you're some sort of spy," I whispered. He chuckled softly and faced forward.

The presentation began, and we watched in silence as they unveiled a white machine that looked like a sewing machine-loom hybrid. Of course, it wasn't life-sized, but that didn't seem to dampen the excitement of the inventor. Over the next hour, the man explained the different production stages of fabric and how this machine was able to streamline them to create a superior product. Admittedly, it wasn't very interesting, but nothing presented as a PowerPoint ever was.

Cody must have glanced at his watch five times. I fully expected him to walk out in the middle of the presentation like he'd done in Milan when we saw a similar one, but he managed to stay in his seat. When the presentation finished, we clapped and stood to make our way to the exit. As we did, he walked slightly in front of me, turning every so often to make sure I was okay. If the situation were different, it may have been weird, as if the gesture were too intimate. Since there was no way anyone would be interested in an enormously pregnant woman unless it was the man who'd made her that way, which he wasn't, I knew he was just being a good friend.

CHAPTER TWO

ROWAN

I SPOTTED her the minute she walked into the room. She was impossible to miss, with a laugh that lit up the place. I had a feeling she'd be in this conference, but because Fashion Week was about to launch, I wasn't sure I'd get a chance to see her. I had, and I regretted ever wanting to. There was a burn in the middle of my chest that remained as I watched her speak to a familiar-looking man. I couldn't place him, but I knew him, and I hated him. I hated the protective way in which he held her as he pulled her through the crowd. I hated the way in which he looked at her while she spoke, as if the sun hung on each word she said. I hated the way it ripped me apart, and I hated that I was to blame for it all.

My heart launched into my throat as they neared. I wondered if she'd see me then. She didn't. She laughed again at something he said into her ear. I let my gaze slide down her and saw her bulging belly. It wasn't big, but she was obviously pregnant. How far along? I couldn't tell. My eyes snapped up to her face, to his. They both looked elated, his hand on her stomach as they spoke. Agony clawed at my throat. I managed to push it down and turn to the woman beside me.

"How far along do you think she is?"

The woman's brows pulled in slightly. We'd just been talking about fabric and elasticity, so it wasn't as if my out-of-left-field question was completely ludicrous to ask. She examined Tessa for a moment before shrugging. "It's hard to tell. Maybe six months? I think I looked about that size at around six months."

"Thank you."

Six months? I typed furiously into the search engine on my phone, looking for photos of pregnant women and how far along they were. I compared her to before and after photos of women who were as skinny as she was. According to Google, she must have been maybe five months along. Thinner women showed faster was what the explanations on the message boards stated. Fucking message boards.

How had she moved on so quickly?

How had she moved on at all?

I hadn't.

I'd finally pulled myself out of the drunken stupor I'd been in from the moment I let her go. I wasn't proud of it in the least.

It had been seven months and I was just now pulling myself together and working on what I set out to do—make Hawthorne Industries a household name. I had a plan. A plan that included buying back the company, filing for divorce, and going after my girl. The longer I stood there and watched her with her preppy, blond baby daddy, the more I doubted anything at all coming of my plan. What would I do? Waltz up there and take her from him, caveman style? Demand that she come with me when she was pregnant with his child? No. I'd lost her. My throat closed up at the realization.

I spent the next hour watching them, and when it was over, I idled and watched them interact with others. I could walk up to her and say hi. She'd be socially forced to tell me about the relationship and the baby. I'd do the math. Figure out how long it's been since she decided to move on. It would be unfair, though, which was why I couldn't do it. My brother was arriving soon, anyway. I was sure he knew about it and hadn't told me because he didn't want to hurt me.

It wouldn't be fair to walk into her life when I couldn't offer her anything. Besides, I still had almost three years left in my deal with the devil.

I looked up at her one last time, she was nodding at something the woman in front of her was saying. The guy was still at her side, but he was on his phone. Who was he? It didn't matter. The day I let her go, I forfeited the right to question anything about her life. It was the reason I'd thrown my phone into the lake one evening when I was itching to call her and find out how she was doing. It was also why I changed my phone number. A part of me had thought that I would be able to coast through our time apart, knowing she'd be busy trying to create a name for herself in the industry. I hadn't expected *this* though. This was exactly why people said life was a bitch, because she forced you to look at things you fucked up square in the face and deal with them. Life was about making mistakes and having the culmination of those mistakes rubbed in your face continuously. It was where our fight or flight responses kicked in—would you fly or would you fight?

I decided on the former and forced myself to leave the conference.

CHAPTER THREE

TESSA

Eight months later . . .

"I THINK it's cute that you don't think Cody likes you as more than a friend."

"He knows he's just a friend."

I glanced over. No matter what I said, Sam, along with everyone else, automatically paired us together. I'd made it a point to keep Cody at arm's length out of fear that he really did see me as more than a friend. The last thing I wanted or needed was a relationship of any kind. I had a demanding job and a demanding child. That was all I needed.

"A friend who got you pregnant," he stated, rubbing a hand over his short hair and drawing my attention to the scar on the side of his head. It still hurt to think about how he got it. I blinked away from him and looked at the road ahead.

"How are you feeling?" I changed the subject. I loved him too much to have him carry the burden of my truths.

"Good. Tired, but good. I'm hoping with the tests and treatments they want to do to me here I can put this all behind me once and for all. How's the Miles?"

"Good." I smiled, thinking about my little blue-eyed boy and his soothing scent. "So good."

"I can't wait to see him." His smile was so similar to his brother's that it broke my heart a little. He'd only seen the baby on the phone so he hadn't gotten the full effect of Miles's cuteness.

"He's going to love you."

"You think?"

"I know so. You'll be his second favorite uncle." I pursed my lips. "Maybe his first. Freddie doesn't call or FaceTime nearly as often as you do."

He laughed. "Well, I'm glad I'm in the running for the top spot."

"Are you nervous about the treatments?"

I hated asking him the question because I knew it was probably the one thing everyone asked him non-stop, but it was impossible to ignore. Not with his buzz cut or the scar he was sporting, evidence of what he'd gone through to get rid of the tumor.

"I'm hopeful," he said. "They say I'm out of the woods. I just want to make sure I stay that way."

I smiled. "I like that."

"Perks of catching things early and being proactive."

"I'm so glad you did."

"Me too."

I swallowed. "How's your family?"

"Good. Dad's happy. Mom's working on it. Ro's working hard."

Even hearing his nickname made my chest ache. It wasn't that I hadn't moved past our breakup, because I had. It was that every single day with Miles was a reminder of what I was keeping from him, of what he should be part of but I couldn't allow. I also didn't have it in me to complain about the fact that Rowan always seemed to be doing well while I was constantly teetering on the edge of a complete breakdown.

It would be a cold, cold day in hell when I complained to a man who'd just been through brain surgery, though. Absolutely not. It didn't matter that, some days, motherhood was overwhelming because it had no set hours. It didn't matter how frustrated I got or the number of trips I'd had to pass up on because of it, because when I held Miles in my arms nothing else seemed to matter.

"I wouldn't tell you something that would hurt your feelings," he said, seemingly reading the hurt expression on my face.

"The mere acknowledgment of him hurts."

He pressed his lips together. We arrived at my apartment building and parked along the street. Celia and Grandma Joan moved to Paris while I was still pregnant, and we'd upgraded from a one bedroom to a three bedroom. It wasn't a huge place, but it was cozy and the view was to die for.

"How's everything at Prim?" Sam asked as we walked.

"Oh my god. It's awesome. Spectacular. Incredible."

He laughed at my excitement.

"I'm dead serious. Yamina, my boss, keeps talking about the U.S. office that's set to open, and I think she's seriously considering me for a director position." It wasn't anything she'd specifically said, but something in my gut told me that was why she kept bringing it up.

"Where is it going to be?" Sam asked. "In New York?"

"Yeah, that's where they're setting things up."

"That's exciting. I'm happy it's working out for you." We were silent for a moment as we crossed the street. "Are you still sketching dresses during your free time?"

"No. I've been too busy to sketch for pleasure," I said, which wasn't exactly a lie. I had been busy, but there was no way I was telling anyone that I hadn't opened one of my sketchbooks since I had gotten that damn email from Rowan. I hated that a single moment killed my creativity the way it had.

When we got up to the apartment, I opened the door and let Sam walk in before me. He let out a whistle.

"This place is bigger."

I laughed. "Well, we needed more room. It helps when you're rooming with an old rich lady."

Sam smiled.

"Is that Samson I hear?" Grandma Joan called out before she lowered her voice, saying, "Let's go see for ourselves."

She carried Miles in her arms as she approached us. He smiled when he saw me, frowned when he saw Sam. They'd seen each other countless times on the phone, but I was sure it was different for Miles to have him right in front of his face. Sam walked up to him and pinched his chubby cheeks softly.

"Hey, buddy, remember me?" he said in a soft voice that made me smile so hard my cheeks hurt. Miles smiled at him before swinging his tiny arms out toward Sam. I pressed a hand to my chest as Sam gathered him into his arms, kissing my grandmother on the cheek as he did. She held both sides of his face and pulled his forehead to hers.

"I'm so glad you're okay. I've been praying," she said.

"It seems someone heard you." He smiled. Miles held both sides of Sam's face when Joan let go and started to slap him.

"Miles, softly," I said. "Be gentle."

"I can take it." Sam laughed looking at Miles. "You trying to beat your uncle up?"

Grandma Joan walked over to me with a look of pity on her face. When she reached me, she brought her hands to my face and brushed my cheeks. "Get a hold of yourself, sweetheart."

I hadn't even realized I'd been crying, but the ache in my chest seemed to tighten. I blinked and nodded, excusing myself to use the restroom. I was so thrilled to have Sam here, but it made me think about Rowan and what seeing Miles would do to him. What would he say? What would he think?

When I couldn't hide anymore, I splashed cold water on my face, took a deep breath and walked back out. Sam was walking in slow circles as he examined Miles as he carried him, scanning his little face. Was it me or was he looking a little too closely? He glanced up at me, giving me a long look. I held my breath. What if he knew? He glanced back at Miles and continued to coo at him. I felt myself breathe a little easier. I wasn't sure what I'd do if Samson asked me outright about Miles's father. He seemed pretty convinced it was Cody, and I hoped that for Miles's sake it stayed that way, because I didn't really want to imagine having my son around Camryn while I wasn't around.

CHAPTER FOUR

ROWAN

Rowan

It had been one year to the day when I saw Tessa again, this time in London. I was speaking to my mother, Camryn, and a woman from a well-known fashion magazine when she walked through the doors of the convention center. My breath caught at the sight of her, or maybe it was an exhale, because for the first time in a long time, I felt like I could breathe. Her brown hair was down in long, shiny waves that I longed to run my hands through. The form-fitting plum dress hugged all her curves, which didn't even hint at her having had a baby.

Baby.

My breath caught for an entirely different reason, and I looked behind her, around her, but she was alone.

Not wanting to alert my mother or Camryn of her arrival, I tore my gaze from her and joined the conversation again. I kept my eyes on Camryn's profile. She was in a good mood, the way she often was in this setting, when my attention was mostly on her. It was the only time my attention was ever on her. Over the last two years, the seed of animosity I felt for her had grown into a damn rainforest.

Camryn could pretend all she wanted, but she was as miserable as I was. She reminded me of it every night as she drowned in her wine or when she was leaving to spend the night at her boyfriend's apartment on Madison. She'd rekindled her relationship with him recently, stating that she couldn't bear the sight of me or the new beard I'd grown.

"You're letting yourself go," she'd said. "You're letting yourself go because of that stupid bitch."

That was after she tried everything she could think of to make me react to the fact that she was having an affair. From sending pictures of them together to showing up at restaurants with him where she knew I'd be hosting meetings. We hadn't exactly stated terms that we couldn't sleep with other people while we were married, so technically, she wasn't violating the agreement we had and she wasn't overly obvious about the affair in public.

I lifted my gaze and scanned the room, finding Tessa again. Her back was facing me, but the woman she was talking to had her full attention. Whatever Tessa was saying must have been worth listening to. I wanted so badly to know what it was. To trade places with that lady and have a moment alone with Tessa. One moment was all I needed. One moment to beg for forgiveness. To ask if we could remain friends. We'd remained friends after we broke up and left for college, and until Hawthorne Industries took over her family's company, we'd been fine. Yes, this was different. We'd slept together and broke up because I was getting married, but we could still be friends. People remained friends all the time. Why couldn't we? The thought of seeing her with another man flashed through my mind once more, and I knew why I couldn't completely pull it off. Seeing her with someone else would kill me.

The next three hours were spent in and out of conference rooms and shows. My mother checked out after the second one, leaving Camryn and me behind to attend the rest of the conference.

"I'm going to go find a bar," she said after the second demonstration.

"I'll be here until it ends." I looked down at my pamphlet. The next presentation was aimed at giving companies run by women in third world countries a chance to get their fabrics out there, and I actually wanted to hear her pitch.

She sighed. "Haven't we seen enough fabric for one weekend?"

"No."

"Come on, let's skip the rest. You can get the details from the pamphlet if you want to contact anyone." She put her hand on my forearm and looked up at me, her lips forming a smirk as her eyes twinkled. "I'll make it worthwhile."

I raised an eyebrow. It didn't matter that I hadn't had sex in a long time. *Too long.* The thought of touching this woman was revolting to me. "I'll call you when I'm finished. We can have dinner with my mother."

"Okay." She shrugged a bony shoulder before leaning in and kissing me.

I broke away before she could deepen the kiss and turned, not waiting for her to walk away before I went into the next room. It was set up classroom style, with small tables that sat two people. I took a seat and listened to the pitch, but my head wasn't completely in it. I kept looking around, waiting, wondering if I'd spot Tessa again. It wasn't until it was over that I saw her off to the right, sitting on her own. I headed that way, heart pounding in my chest. She lifted her head as if sensing my presence, her eyes widening when she saw me.

"Is this seat taken?"

She shook her head, still looking at me as if she wasn't sure whether I was really in front of her. I undid the button of my suit and sat beside her.

"You look well."

"You too," she whispered, blinking and tearing her eyes away from me. I still saw the tears gathering on her lashes.

"I'm sorry."

"What are you apologizing for?"

"Everything."

"Specifically, what are you apologizing for?"

My heart stopped beating for a second when she met my gaze. "I hurt you. I didn't want to."

"Are you saying that because you regret the decision you made?"

"Every day for the last two years."

"I'm not ready to forgive you."

"That's fair." I exhaled, wondering if I should bring up the fact that I saw her while she was pregnant, saw her boyfriend. Instead, I asked, "Are you happy?"

"I am." She turned a slow but genuine smile in my direction. It was the smile I had always chased, the one she gave Sam so freely but had kept from me for years. It was so beautiful that it made me jolt every time I saw it. "Very happy."

So, I did the right thing letting you go, I wanted to say. *I did the right thing by letting you walk away from me and right into his arms.* I couldn't, though, because my voice was suddenly stuck beneath a boulder in my throat. I put my hand over hers on the table and squeezed it. She let me. Then I stood and walked away, letting her bask in her happiness. I owed her that much.

CHAPTER FIVE

ROWAN

Two years later . . .

"I HATE YOU."

I dodged a second plate thrown in my direction. Heart pounding in my ears, I stalked up to Camryn in the kitchen and grabbed her by the shoulders. "You need to get the hell out of my house."

She took my nearness as an invitation to lean forward and try to kiss me. I turned my face to the side. Her lips landed on my jaw, which stiffened. I held her farther away from me.

"I hate you," she cried. "You're a stupid, emotionless son of a bitch, and I hate you."

I looked at her. "Are you done?"

"Why can't you change?" she asked between sobs, her body shaking but I still didn't give. If I gave Camryn an inch, she'd take a yard. For four years, I'd managed to steer clear of anything that would ignite any idea that this could turn into something more and I wasn't about to give when I was so close to being free of her.

"I can't change because I don't love you," I said simply. "What's brought this on? Did Roger decide to leave you?"

She narrowed her eyes, yanking herself away from my grasp. "Don't talk about my relationship with Roger as if you give a shit about me or my emotions. If you cared so much, I wouldn't have been with him to begin with."

"I'm asking as a friend."

"Well, I don't need a fucking friend." She turned around, picked up her purse, and stormed out of the kitchen.

"I need you to get your things out of the closet and make this move official," I called out.

"Fuck you, Rowan." She slammed the door loudly.

I closed my eyes and pinched the bridge of my nose, wondering how the fuck I got here. My brother had warned me that I'd be miserable. Tessa warned me that I'd be miserable. Hell, I had known I would be miserable. Still, a part of me figured I would be able to handle it, that it wouldn't be that bad. Work had kept me busy enough most of the time to keep my mind off all of this, but occasionally, on the weekends when Camryn was out with her friends and I was out with mine, I couldn't help but wonder what life would be like with a partner. A real partner, one who would share the good and the bad with me, not just ask questions with dollar signs in her eyes. It wasn't her fault she was like that. It also wasn't her fault that she prioritized the New York nightlife over everything else. I'd made it that way. I'd pushed her away so completely and let her believe there was no room in my life for a sidekick. Truth was, I had room in my life. I just didn't want her to fill that space.

I picked up my keys and called the nearest locksmith before heading to the bar where I was set to meet my brother.

When I walked into the hole-in-the-wall bar, I walked straight toward my brother, who was sitting by the window, looking at the people walking by. It was a busier weekday than usual here in Brooklyn, with the new art galleries opening around the corner and everyone gearing up for a busy spring. Sam looked up when I reached the table and sat across from him.

"Still sporting a beard *and* now you're dressing down?" He smiled. "Brooklyn's rubbing off on you."

"I'm trying to turn over a new leaf." Truth was, I'd been sporting the beard for a while. What started as a November challenge developed into a newfound love of having hair on my face.

"What does your wife think about this leaf you're turning?"

"The wife I kicked out this morning? She probably hates it."

Sam chuckled. "What did she say when you told her to move out?"

"Threw a plate at my head."

"Shit." Sam cringed over a chuckle. "That bad? What does she expect? She barely lives there anyway."

"Right, but my being the one to kick her out makes her feel like she holds no control over the situation." I shrugged. "You know Camryn."

"A raging bitch? Yeah," Sam said.

I shrugged. Couldn't argue there.

"Have you spoken to Mom?" he asked, humor twinkling his eyes.

"You're an asshole, you know that?" I picked up a fry from the sharing plate in the middle of the table and threw it at him. He laughed, catching it before it hit him in the face.

"I'm just asking. She seems to have a soft spot for Camryn. She must really play it up for her."

"Not much to play up. I'm sure she runs and tells Mom what a dick I am and how I don't love her or show her I care about her and Mom immediately identifies." The waitress came back to set down another appetizer Sam had ordered and I ordered a beer. "Mom showed me who her priority was."

"I hope you aren't directing that statement at me," he said, lifting an eyebrow. "You know she only calls me because she feels like she almost lost me, not because I'm her favorite."

"I never wanted to be her favorite."

"Mister Perfect never wanted his parents' approval?" He raised both eyebrows this time. I threw another fry at him, laughing as my beer was set in front of me.

Our mother and I had a series of differences these last few years, and each one had created another barrier between us. We still spoke, but not nearly as often as she and Sam spoke and definitely not nearly as often as she spoke to Camryn, whom she seemed to speak to every few days according to the texts my mom sent me.

"Are you ready for a rebound yet?"

I shook my head, taking a sip of beer. I wasn't sure whom I would be rebounding. Camryn? That would be a joke considering I was never actually with her. As usual, all thoughts turned to Tessa. Some people were impossible to get over. You could make yourself move past them, but deep down you knew you'd never fully be rid of them.

"You're right. I don't think even you could pull a woman right now. You're a bore when you go out," he added, holding back a laugh. I shot him an unamused look. "You are. You're always checking your phone, looking at the time, talking about how early you need to be up."

"Yeah, well, it's part of the whole being an adult gig."

"Like I said, boring."

I chuckled. "You're an idiot."

He smiled. "What happened to the brunette? Mayra? She was cute."

"Mayra was a one-time thing. You know that."

Since letting Tessa walk away, I'd only slept with two women. One had been Camryn, a mistake I'd never let myself live down, and the other had been Mayra, the one-night stand, which by definition was a mistake. It wasn't that I didn't enjoy sex these days but sleeping with them had made it clear that I didn't just want any woman who would spread her legs for me. I wanted to feel what I'd felt with Tessa and recreating that was impossible.

I'd gladly taken a break from women and focused on the company and on my brother's health. The last three years had brought us closer than I imagined we would be. Seeing him go through his cancer diagnosis and treatment had really put things into perspective for both of us. Our grandfather had been diagnosed with the same cancer when we were young, but it was different seeing someone you saw as an old man go through it. Seeing your own brother was a tough pill to swallow—the weight loss, the mood swings, both the visible and invisible scars, the defeat in his eyes some days. I'd put all of my energy into being there for him. I couldn't take the diagnosis from him or do his treatments for him, but I could hold his hand through it all. And here we were. He was healthy, happy, with a new outlook on life. Most days, that was all I needed in order to continue with my own life as if I hadn't been affected by his struggle. Sam leaned back in his seat and ran a hand through his hair. I watched the movement, wondering how it must feel to touch all that hair after not having any at all.

"What'd you want to talk about?"

"The future of the company."

He thrummed his fingers on the table, watching me. I'd been working tirelessly not only on expanding it but also on ways to buy it from our grandparents and uncle.

"You mean the accounts in Colombia and Paraguay?"

"No." I exhaled heavily. "They are still refusing to talk to me because I'm a man and their priority is working with women business owners.

"I thought one of the points of marrying Camryn was so she'd put up a face for the company."

I scoffed. "If I send her anywhere near those women, I really won't stand a chance at getting those fabrics."

"Send someone else. What about Rosa?"

I shook my head. "She just had a baby. She won't be back for at least two months."

"Erin?"

"Too blonde, too skinny."

"But unlike Camryn, Erin has a soul."

I laughed because he was right. "Still." I shook the idea away. "I can't send her. Maybe this is a blessing in disguise. I've already waited this long. I need to focus on other things, which is what I want to talk to you about."

"Okay." He frowned and put a healthy portion of his Paratha —an Indian flatbread—in his mouth, chewing it slowly as he watched me.

"I'm buying the company and dissolving the board. I told the lawyer to draft the new contract so that it's a fifty-fifty partnership."

He stopped chewing, eyes wide. "Camryn?"

"Hell no." I leaned forward, making sure I had his undivided attention. "You and me."

"But . . . this company is your dream. You were the one who sold your soul to the devil, literally, to get it. I didn't do anything."

"You work just as hard as I do." I smiled when he gave me an incredulous look. "Fine, *almost* as hard as I do."

It wasn't that he didn't work his ass off. It was just completely different work. Where I had nearly four hundred people to oversee, Sam had twenty. It didn't matter. I took advantage of his clearly speechless state to continue my explanation.

"I don't want this to be a company that we hand down to your kids with contingencies. I want this to be a partnership, an equal partnership between two brothers. The creative team you've built has been doing incredible things for Hawthorne Industries. We can rebrand, make it what we want it to be."

"Rebranding could take a while."

"We have time."

Our clientele had expanded from furniture to clothing and beyond. I wanted to continue expanding and rebranding may help us get there. Our main plates came and we dug into those.

"You said my kids," Sam said suddenly.

I paused mid-chew. "What?"

"You said to hand down to my kids. What about yours?"

I smiled, shaking my head. "I'm not going to have kids."

"And you think I am?"

"You have a heart of gold, Samson. Fuck yes, you'll have kids."

"I don't even know if I'm fertile after all the shit they injected into me."

I swallowed the agony that crawled into my throat as I thought about his treatments and everything they'd taken from him. Somehow, he'd made it out stronger and better while I crumbled with the weight of the worry.

"What do the doctors say?"

"That it's possible, but not likely," he said. "They'd have to check my sperm count again, but it isn't like I'm jumping into fatherhood anytime soon. I bought my own place, and that's enough adulting for me."

I smiled. He'd made his first big purchase and moved into a building in Dumbo. I'd chosen a Brownstone a block over from him, but I wasn't sold on it. Too many rooms, too many renovations to be done. Camryn hated Brooklyn, which was why I closed on the house. It was petty, I knew it was, but I had still done it.

"What's going on with Chloe?" I asked. "Only you would end up in a long-distance relationship."

"Yeah, well, long-distance no more. She's moving here in a month."

"What? You didn't tell me. It's that serious?"

He shrugged, still smiling. "Only time will tell. She's working for Tessa."

The name slammed into me like a ball to left field. "Tessa's coming here?"

Freaking crickets. Nope. He wasn't getting away with that crap.

"Sam. Is Tessa moving back?"

He chuckled, looking over. "You can't let things go, can you?"

"You know I'm nosey."

"Not that nosey." I just waited. "Fine. Yes, she's coming back to New York and running the Prim office here."

I nodded, shoving my emotions so deep not even a molecule of light hit them.

When it came to Tessa, I was more than nosey. I had followed her career. I had paid attention to what her siblings were up to. I found out everything about the man she had a child with. Cody Maverick.

That was the blow that had almost dropped me. He worked with major department stores, buying clothes from fashion designers and stocking them. I'd met him when Tessa and I had gone to the city for meetings. Apparently, she had seen him as something more than a business contact because she hadn't had an issue with jumping into bed with him. The memories still clawed at me, keeping me up at night until I remind myself that I had slept with Camryn the night we got married. I didn't have a damn leg to stand on.

"Well, I'm happy for her." I cleared my throat. "Let's get back to the topic. Are you ready to make this a partnership? We'll change the name, renew the brand to our liking. You've already taken the leadership role in the creative department. Your responsibilities don't have to change unless you feel like you're ready to take on more."

Sam sat back and considered me. After a long pause, he said, "You know what? Let's do it."

"Let's do it."

CHAPTER SIX

TESSA

THE FIRST REACTION I had to my brand-spanking-new office was to squeal and jump like a lunatic. It was a corner office in a New York City sky-rise. Never in a billion trillion years had I dreamed I'd ever be able to call a place like this mine. Well, sort of mine. It was Prim's, but as the new creative director of the U.S. offices, it was kind of mine. I squealed again, which had Chloe bursting into laughter.

"This place is heaven."

"I know, right?" I was smiling so hard my cheeks hurt. "I have to bring Miles one of these days. Hell, I have to bring Celia, Freddie, and my grandma one of these days."

Chloe was still laughing as she walked over to the floor-to-ceiling windows, but then she sighed dreamily. "My god, this view."

"How am I supposed to get any work done here?" I asked. "I mean, real talk, how?"

"Hell, if I know." She pressed the side of her face to the window and looked at me. "Is this weird? Because it feels so good and you can't hear any noise."

I ran to join her and pressed my own ear against the window. "Nope. Not weird at all." We were definitely acting like children, but it didn't matter. When Yamina gave me the news that I'd gotten the promotion and would be opening the position as the very first creative director in the New York office, I'd cried, and cried, and then begged to take Chloe with me. Not just because she and Sam had started this long-distance relationship that was making even me suffer from anxiety, but because she was a kickass assistant, and I knew one day she'd be so much more than that for this company. Chloe backed away from the window and held her phone up so she could take a selfie as she made a silly face before looking at me.

"Stand behind the desk. I need to send Sam a picture of this."

I laughed and obliged, adopting the most boss-like poses I could summon—both my fists on the desk with a serious face and then my arms crossed with a smile on my face.

"I feel like I'm doing Glamour Shots," I said between laughs. Chloe was laughing equally as hard as she fired away the texts.

"He's going to flip out."

"Miles is going to flip out." My smile widened as I thought of him.

"When are you going to bring him?"

"I'm not sure." I looked around the office again, taking note of the electrical outlets I'd have to plug before his visit. He wasn't a tiny baby anymore, but he loved those outlets.

Chloe's phone vibrated in her hand. She laughed as she answered. "Babe, did you see? No. No. That's Tessa's new office! Yes! Yes! Hold on." She walked over and handed me her phone before telling me she would be right back.

I lifted the phone to my ear. "Hello, peasant."

Sam chuckled. "I hope you know I'm moving into that office."

"We'll have to be roommates because I don't ever want to leave."

"When are you bringing Miles? I wanna be there when he sees it."

"I was just saying that to Chlo. I don't know. Maybe Friday after I pick him up from school?" Calling his daycare a school wasn't a stretch of the imagination since he really was in a school-like environment.

"Text me and I'll be there. Did you find babysitting for next Saturday?"

"For the bar opening? You know it."

Sam's friend was opening up a bar in Brooklyn and Sam had designed the entire concept. I was more than a little excited to see it come to fruition.

"Fantastic. I have to run, but your office is amazing. Tell Chloe to call me when she leaves."

"I will. See you Saturday."

We finished the call and I set the phone down, smiling at the picture of Sam and Chloe that she had saved as her backdrop. They were in front of the Eiffel Tower. Her pretty blonde hair was covering half his face as she kissed his cheek, her arms thrown over his shoulders.

The phone screen went to black right as Chloe walked back in with three white tubes tucked under one arm. I shrugged off the navy-blue blazer I had on and tossed it on the sleek gray couch beside my desk before turning back to Chloe, who was back to looking around with a goofy smile on her face.

"Show me what you got, *mon cherie*."

"We have a few projects happening at once," she said, opening the first tube and unrolling the blueprint on the table.

"What—" I blinked rapidly and looked at Chloe. "Are you sure this is the right thing?"

"It has your name on it." She turned over the tube to show me.

"It's a car."

She chewed on the tip of her fingernail, looking at the blueprint. "I know. Yamina didn't say anything about this to you?"

"No."

I stared at it for a couple of beats longer before pulling the binder that accompanied it toward me and leafing through it. In my time working at Prim, I'd mostly focused on high fashion with the exception of a luxury jet I'd helped design last year, which was not in any way ordinary for me. The company had many branches, but high fashion and interior design for luxury spaces were the two we focused on most. Luxury spaces meaning homes for the rich and famous and sometimes boutique hotels. Cars weren't something we saw often. I looked at the other binder on the desk and noticed that it was a hotel. The third binder was more my style—the spring line for a popular designer.

"A car and a hotel." I let out a breath. "No pressure."

Chloe let out a nervous laugh. "I know."

I opened the fourth binder, which was much smaller and contained some amateur-looking sock designs. "I don't get it."

"What do you mean?"

"Whose designs are these?" I glanced at the bottom of the page and saw RHS Designs. "Never heard of them."

"Me either," Chloe mused, frowning. "Actually, they sound

familiar. Maybe we worked with them in Paris? I have to check my notes."

"Do they want us to pick their fabrics? Design more? I'm so confused."

"I'll get more details. What I have so far is that they want us using the same textiles company for all of the projects," she said. "The car is for Fashion Week. They want to put it in the middle of a runway show."

"Sounds . . . interesting?"

"Yeah. The hotel is a project we need to put a bid on. Best design for the lobby and downstairs bar wins and gets to design the entire hotel, rooms included. It's a small boutique in BK."

BK. She said it the way people spoke about the food chain.

"I'm glad one of us is hip enough to say BK when talking about Brooklyn."

"You're hip." She smiled. "Besides, my college roommate was from BK, and that was all I heard for the four years I roomed with her. I'm going to finish pulling the information for the meeting with the textiles company. Do you want me to have Seth and Tommy work on some of these designs?"

"Send them the car and the boutique. Both companies know exactly what look they're going for, so that shouldn't be too difficult. I'll keep the socks and the spring collection for now. I assume they want designs that match the two they sent us. I think I can come up with ten more."

"Perfect," she said before grabbing the paperwork for the two projects I was delegating and walking out of the office.

I pushed off the table and walked behind my desk, pushing the button on my phone that would speed dial the Paris office, specifically Yamina's.

"*Bonjour*, Cristophe. *Je dois parler à Yamina.*"

"CRISTOPHE, *bonjour*! May I please speak with Yamina if she's available?"

"Of course," he said, switching to his heavily accented English before he put me on hold. Three songs later, Yamina picked up the line.

"Tessa, are you calling to tell me how much you love the new office?"

I laughed. "Well, I don't think the view is quite good enough, but it will do. I actually have a question about the upcoming projects."

"Ask away."

"I'm staring at a blueprint of a car and another of a hotel," I said. "This isn't my department."

Yamina let out a throaty laugh. "Everything is your department now, dear. It's creative, and you're the director."

"But it's a car," I said quietly. "And a hotel."

"And I trust you'll know how to delegate those tasks to others. What I will not allow is for you to sell yourself short. Do you remember why I put you in that position?"

"Because I'm the best." She'd told me that so many times that I'd started to believe her along the way.

"Yes."

"Okay." I nodded to myself. She was right. I'd worked on different things that didn't only include dresses. I could do this. "So, we're working on a boutique hotel, a car, a spring collection for Vue, and socks?"

"We're bidding to work on a boutique hotel, the car is a definite yes, they want Prim-level talent."

"No pressure," I said. "What about the socks?"

"The textiles company we're using is giving us the biggest discount I've ever seen for the other projects as long as we help them design those socks."

"That is—"

"Business," Yamina said. "Just do the same thing you do when we work on handbags or couches or carpets for private jets."

"This is insane."

"It is. Go make me proud and send everyone my best. Call me if you need anything."

For a few long seconds after she hung up, I stood there speechless. Then I set the phone back on the cradle and sighed. A boutique hotel, a car, spring dresses, and socks it was.

CHAPTER SEVEN

MILES HOPPED OFF HIS BED, climbed back on, and did it again. Thank god for small luxuries like toddler beds.

"Get your book," I said. "Where is it?"

"I dunno." He did a one-eighty turn and shrugged. "Let's use the telescope."

I loved it when he said that word. Tele-sh-scope. He hopped onto the bed again. I sighed, folding the last pair of socks I could find a match for and tossing them in the drawer. I picked up six lone socks and shook my head. I'd literally just purchased a new bag of socks for this very reason.

"Te-lesh-scope," Miles said again, slowly this time.

"There are too many lights in the city, babe. I'll have to take you upstate so you can see the stars. Maybe we can stay at Nana Joan's house and set up the telescope there."

He'd gotten a telescope for Christmas and hadn't been able to really use it. Leave it to my son to even know what that was, let alone what it was used for. I blamed Freddie for Mile's obsession with everything NASA. He'd even painted Miles's room blue before putting stars on the ceiling and rockets on the walls. It looked like an astronaut's dream. Or nightmare. I wasn't entirely sure which.

"Nana Joan is coming tomorrow," Miles said.

"She is." I smiled up at him. "Are you excited?"

He nodded, wide smile on his face. Miles loved my mom, but Grandma Joan was his favorite. Probably because Mom tried to be authoritative and Grandma Joan let him do whatever his little heart desired. It wasn't difficult. All he had to do was bat those pretty, incredibly long eyelashes and flash that smile. I couldn't blame her for it. More often than not, I had to catch myself before I gave in to one of his unnecessary demands.

"Miles? Tess?" Celia called out.

"In Miles's room," I called back, but Miles was already rushing out of the room in search of his aunt.

In an effort to live together but still feel like we had our own spaces, we'd found this incredible place in Dumbo. The owners we were renting from had purchased three big apartments on the seventh floor of the building years before Dumbo became a popular place to live. They hoped that their children and their families would one day move into them. When that didn't happen, they rented the space.

I was on the floor folding the rest of Miles's clothes when Celia walked in with him in her arms.

"Miles says he wants to use the telescope Eddie bought him."

She stifled a laugh. I bit my lip to hold back my own. Miles used to call Freddie Eddie because he couldn't pronounce his name properly. He'd moved past it and started saying it correctly, but Celia and I used it to torment Freddie all the time.

"Eddie's gonna be so happy to hear that," I said.

Miles sighed, shimmying out of Celia's hold. "I said Freddie."

We laughed lightly. I extended my arms and grabbed Miles as he tried to run past me, bringing him to my chest in a tight hug and kissing his chubby cheeks over and over. "I just love you so much."

He giggled in my arms and broke free to walk back over to the telescope.

"You actually put it together for him?" Celia took a seat across from me and grabbed a shirt to fold.

"No, dude. He did it himself." I looked over at him. "I know I'm his mom and all, but I swear that kid is a genius."

"He is. Who else learns to read at two years old?"

"Excuse me." I threw a shirt at her face, laughing at the look on her face. "I learned to read at two."

"Yeah, but you're a girl. Boys are slower than girls."

I laughed. "You didn't know how to read at two and you're a girl."

"Freddie was super slow." She stuck her tongue out.

"And Freddie's a boy."

She threw the shirt back at my face. I laughed as I caught it.

"You look tired," she commented.

"I am."

I was so exhausted from the long week. Between work and Miles's after daycare activities, I was drained. We'd been working on the bid for the hotel and had some sock designs, but the car was a pain in the ass, mainly because we kept looking at past designs and were trying to come up with a cool, new concept. To add to the stress, the director of acquisitions, Ryan Ford, was on vacation. Who took a vacation the week they started a high-paying job? A man. That was who.

"Why don't you go shower and change, and I'll finish folding and putting away his clothes and tuck him in tonight?"

My shoulders slumped in relief, letting out some of the stress they'd been holding. I tilted my neck back and forth, hoping to alleviate the pain there.

"You'd be a total lifesaver. I'll tuck him in, though." I smiled. Tucking him in was my favorite part of the job.

ONCE I WAS SHOWERED, I felt refreshed. I picked up some scattered toys on my way over to Miles's room and stood at the doorway just as Celia was finishing *The Giving Tree*. It was impossible for me to read that book and not get choked up, and apparently, she felt the same way. Walking over to them, I shut off his lights and turned on the nightlight by his bed, as Celia closed the book, gave him a kiss, and stood. I crouched and gave him another.

"Did you use the restroom?"

He nodded.

"I mean in the last ten minutes, have you used it?"

"No."

"Miles! Please do that now." I uncovered him and watched him walk to the bathroom across the hall. I'd do anything for my child, but if I could avoid washing the sheets again, that would be awesome. Once he was back in bed, I pulled his covers up around him, gave him another kiss, and said good night.

Celia and I walked out in silence, waiting until we were in the kitchen to speak.

"Are we going out on Saturday?" she asked.

"I told Sam we would, but ugh."

"Ugh, nothing. You haven't gone anywhere since we moved here, and I specifically remember you blaming your lack of a love life on not having someone to watch Miles. Lo and behold, you now have Freddie and me plus Grandma Joan and Mom who are coming tomorrow, so no excuses."

I grabbed us each a glass of wine. "I never said anything about my lack of a love life. That was you. Even if I did want a love life, I don't plan on meeting anyone at this bar slash restaurant slash lounge or whatever it is. I'm going because Sam had a hand in designing it. That's it. Maybe you should worry about your own non-existent love life."

"That's different," she said before taking a sip of wine. "*I've* decided to take a year of celibacy. I think everyone can appreciate that cleanse. You've had almost four years. You're overdue."

"It hasn't been four, stop being dramatic."

"I'm not saying you haven't been busy, but now you have this awesome, lucrative position with an equally awesome office, and this great kid and . . . I don't know. Don't you feel like it's time?"

I took a sip of my wine and then set the glass on the counter, running my finger along the rim. "I hooked up with that French guy, remember?"

"Oh my god. Stop. We said we wouldn't count that." She laughed. I felt myself smile. It had been a mess. "What about Cody? Have you spoken to him?"

"Cody and I are friends. Nothing more, and no I haven't spoken to him. He knows we're here, but I'd rather keep things as platonic as possible."

"Because you don't want to lead him on."

"Exactly."

"That guy would trip over his feet if you gave him a shot."

"I like him standing. Thanks."

"Uh-huh."

"Fine." I huffed. "It isn't that he isn't a great catch. He has it all. I just don't see him in that way." It was like Sam all over again.

"You definitely have a type," she said. "Cody doesn't have the build to qualify."

I laughed. "By type, I don't mean body type."

"He isn't alpha enough for you."

I scrunched my nose. He wasn't. "But he is cute. He's more your type."

"God no. He's too much of a goody-two-shoes."

I laughed. "Speaking of bad boys, have you spoken to Ben again after he called a few weeks ago?"

"He called again the other day. I didn't answer."

"Why not?" I couldn't understand her. Every time she had a little bit of wine in her she'd talk about Ben with regret in her voice. He was a super successful soccer player. Super hot. Super rich. Super . . . male. He was totally up her alley, with his tattoos and his sexy smirk.

"All those things you just listed." She raised an eyebrow. "They seem like pros until you're in a relationship with the guy. Then all of those things that attracted you in the first place become all of the things that make you self-conscious."

"Because of the girls?"

"I think that's a big part of it. The whole larger-than-life existence those people have . . ." She shook her head. "Imagine these baseball players and American football players? Multiply that by a million. Their football is in a league of its own. They get hit on by women from every single country, every single town, every single . . . it's too much. I can't handle it."

"It's been great for your poetry, though."

"Hell yeah." She laughed and then sobered. "So, have you thought about telling Rowan?"

"No." My chest squeezed. "I mean, yes, I've thought about it and thought about it and thought about it, but I can't. It would be a horrible idea."

"I get it. I mean, I can see the pros and cons, but I get it."

"I can't hide him forever," I said. "I don't *want* to hide him forever, I just can't think of the right time to tell him. What would I do? Show up at his doorstep?"

Celia shrugged as if she didn't know what to say. We fell into a comfortable silence, finished off our wine, and washed the glasses before saying good night.

On my way to bed, I peeked into Miles's room one last time, watching the way his little chest rose and fell. A part of me was dying to tell Rowan because I felt guilty. I knew it was wrong for me to keep something this big to myself, but then I remembered Camry and Mildred and I stopped myself every time.

Telling Rowan would mean those women would be in my son's life, and that was something I couldn't tolerate. There was no way I would let them poison the sweetness Miles had.

Did it make me selfish? Yes. Did it make me wrong? Probably. Did I give a shit? No. This was my son's wellbeing, and it was something I didn't have to debate with anyone.

CHAPTER EIGHT

TESSA

I'D BEEN on the phone with Ryan Ford the entire morning. His flight had been delayed, so instead of canceling the meetings, we'd conferenced in the marketing director and the accounting department to update everyone on this week's agenda and key performance indicators. Chloe knocked on the door and peeked her head in just as I was hanging up the phone with him. Her brows rose when she took in the expression on my face.

"Uh-oh. Should I have listened in on that call to take notes?"

"He'll be in and out of the office tomorrow, but I have to take over the meeting with the sock company. He's emailing me details as we speak, and . . . I think that's basically it. How are Seth and Tommy coming along on the car and hotel?"

"They already finalized the leather for the car. They want your input on the design when you get a chance." She jotted everything down on her digital clipboard and looked up when she was done. "They are still waiting on the files from marketing to see what the rest of the hotels look like. Since we have to bid to work on it, they are obviously looking for something different."

"Agreed." I leaned my head against my chair and closed my eyes, letting the to-do list run rampant in my mind.

"Rumor has it the owner of the hotel is Ryan Ford's brother."

My eyes popped open. "How do you know this? And why would Ryan work here if his family is in the hotel business?"

"No clue. Like I said, it's just a rumor around the break room." She smiled. "You know, the place lowly employees hang out in."

"Shut up." I clicked on the email from Ryan and forwarded it to Chloe.

She laughed as she stood. "I'm going to go confirm the meeting for today and then I'll let Seth know."

"Perfect."

We'd be using the same textiles company for all of our projects, and if I were the one going to those meetings, I'd definitely need to get acquainted with the place. We had three big accounts to focus on, but I had to give the socks attention as well. I was a firm believer that no company was too small to thrive, and if they were taking a chance on us with their fabrics, it was only fair that we take one on them with our designs. Once she left, I got on the phone with marketing so they could fill me in on whatever they'd dug up on the companies and their audience.

Once I was assured I'd have the information by this afternoon, I opened the file Ford had sent me and frowned as I pushed the speaker button and called Chloe.

"Yes?"

"THIS COMPANY HAS NO NAME?"

"Which one? The textiles? I included it in my last email to you."

I clicked on that and froze. "Hawthorne? Are you kidding?"

"Uh, no. I thought you'd be happy. Sam will be there."

I opened my mouth, closed it, opened it, and closed it once more. Sam would be there. So would Rowan if he was in town. Maybe he wasn't. Still, it didn't change the fact that I'd probably have to see him at some point, and wasn't that what I wanted deep down? A way to finally fess up about Miles and take this load off my chest? But not like this. I hadn't really planned on it going over like this.

I was still a nervous wreck on the inside as Chloe, Seth, and I left for the meeting. I had wanted Tommy to come, but Chloe had convinced me that he was better off at the office working on the hotel bid since that was our biggest project.

Seth and Chloe tossed around concepts for the car. I barely paid attention, too consumed with thoughts of seeing Rowan. I'd sent Samson no fewer than ten text messages, all of which went unanswered.

"What about apples? Too corny?" Chloe asked.

I blinked. "Corny."

"Not good," Seth agreed.

Chloe took out her clipboard and made a note.

"Do you take that thing everywhere?" Seth asked.

"Everywhere," I said.

"That is not true," Chloe argued.

I looked at Seth and whispered, "Everywhere."

He chuckled. Chloe rolled her eyes but smiled because she

totally did take it everywhere. Not only that. She had two of them—one big and one small.

"Why not just use a smartphone?" Seth asked, waving his One Plus.

"Ew, Android," I said, trying to make my voice normal and get back into the mind frame I'd been in when we left the office.

"Android is so much—"

I put my hand up as we got out of the subway and walked toward the office. Chloe was actually using her phone to map the way. "I know. They update their software all the time and you can download it yourself. I understand the hype. I just don't like it."

"Because it isn't pretty."

"No, because it isn't practical."

Seth scoffed.

"We make a right here," Chloe announced. We followed.

"It is practical. You just said we can update the software," Seth said.

"Yeah, so can I, by doing the update."

"It isn't the same."

"Can we just agree that all phones are awesome because if it weren't for technology we'd be using a legit paper map right now and Seth would be arguing that we were going the wrong way and refusing to ask for directions?" Chloe eyed Seth as he pulled open the door to the building.

When I stepped in, I tried to do as Rowan would have done and shoved my feelings into a box and lock it. It seemed to work as we took the elevator to the fifth floor and exited, but then panic gripped me, tightening its fist around my heart. I may have to work with him and if I did, there wouldn't be any way for me to keep him from finding out about Miles. Again, I reminded myself that it was what I'd wanted. I wanted to tell him. I wanted him to be in Miles's life. I just didn't want her to be in it too. The thought of Camryn hit me like a brick.

"Are you okay?" Chloe asked, grasping my shoulders to steady me. I hadn't realized I'd stumbled.

Samson came rushing from behind her. He placed a hand on her shoulder and gently moved her out of the way so he could take her spot. "I just saw your texts."

"A little late."

"Are you okay?" he asked, his eyes scanning my face. "What's happening? What's the emergency?"

I fought the tears I felt rushing as I looked at him, my dear friend, who'd been there for me when I was down, whom I worried about when he was down, who shipped gifts for Miles and visited him and treated him like his own blood without knowing that he actually was. It wasn't until that very moment that the magnitude of it all hit me. The lies I'd weaved started to wrap around my neck slowly, keeping the truth from spilling out.

"What's wrong?" Sam asked again, concern shining in his eyes. I tried to blink away the tears but blinking only made them trickle down my face quicker.

"I have to tell you something."

He grabbed my arm and ushered me away from Chloe and Seth, down the corridor, and outside the glass doors I'd just walked through. Once we were out of earshot, he faced me.

"What's going on?"

I took a shaky breath and wiped my face. "Miles isn't Cody's."

His eyes widened slightly, his lips parting as he stared at me. After what felt like an eternity, he cleared his throat. "Why are you telling me this now?"

"He's Rowan's." I swallowed the knot in my throat and blinked away briefly, still feeling like I could barely breathe.

"Are you . . . Why didn't you tell me?"

"I couldn't." My stomach started to hurt. I pressed a hand there. "I didn't want Miles anywhere near Camryn or your mother. With me living in another country, I just wasn't sure what . . . I made a mistake," I whispered, wiping new tears. "I'm so sorry. I didn't want to hide it from you, but then you assumed Cody was the father, and I let you because I wasn't ready to tell Ro and I didn't want you to carry this burden."

"You need to tell him, Tessa." His jaw twitched. "He deserves to know."

"I'll do it, I swear I will. I just need time."

"Tessa." Sam heaved a deep breath, covering his face with both his hands before raking them through his hair. "Oh my god."

"I know. I'm so sorry." I reached for his arm, holding him by the wrist. "You know I love you like a brother and Miles thinks of you as an uncle just like Freddie. I was just trying to protect him—"

He dropped his hands and raised his gaze to mine. "This is going to break my brother's heart."

I wanted to argue that, but the tightening in my throat wouldn't ease up. I wanted to remind him that his brother wasn't like us, he didn't feel things the way we did, but there was no use. I didn't know Rowan anymore. For all I knew, the depiction I'd drawn up in my head of him working twenty-four seven and ignoring Miles was wrong. Maybe he'd see Miles and experience the pureness that he brought and decide he wanted to keep him around. It was hard to turn that kind of love away. The unconditional, maddening love that split you in two but made it impossible to live without it. If this had been the other way around, I'd be heartbroken without question.

CHAPTER NINE

ROWAN

THE COMMOTION outside of my office had me heaving a deep sigh before I yanked open the heavy door. Chloe was standing in the hallway next to a guy I didn't know, which was interesting. I had been expecting Prim to send Ford.

"Who are you?"

"Seth. I'm with them," he said by way of explanation as he walked over and shook my hand.

"Rowan," I said, returning the shake.

"I know. I read the article *Times* did on you."

"Ah." I smiled. It seemed like everyone I met lately had read the article.

I looked at the two of them. "Prim sent you for this then?"

"Uh, yeah, but—"

"We're ready," Sam announced as he rounded the corner.

He looked odd, his expression not alight the way it normally was when Chloe was around. I was about to ask who *we* were when Tessa rounded the corner behind him. I sucked in a breath. My heart, which hadn't seemed to function correctly since I'd last seen her, was launched into my throat. I put my hands in my pockets and leaned against the doorframe, watching the way her hips swayed in that wine-colored hip-hugging dress. It should be illegal for her to walk around in that dress. All I could do was picture myself pulling it over her hips—

Jesus.

One look at her and she did this to me.

I needed to focus on something else, but I couldn't stop staring. She looked lethal, self-assured. Confident.

She was a woman who could walk into a meeting with just about anyone and slay. Knowing that person was currently me was both seductive and scary. She stopped in front of me and met my gaze head-on. I cleared my throat, hoping to regain some kind of balance in this situation.

"This is a surprise," I said. It was a lie, but she didn't need to know that.

"For both of us, I can assure you." Those almond-shaped eyes cataloged my features. "You have a beard."

My lips twitched. "Thanks for noticing."

"Kind of impossible not to."

Something bloomed inside me, ran through my blood like wildfire. A sense of belonging I couldn't seem to find anywhere else, and I didn't bother to try to suppress it.

Not this time.

I knew about the kid, but the boyfriend didn't seem like a sure thing. I reminded myself that this was strictly business. I needed her in my corner for the sock company I wanted to open. I straightened, pushed off the frame, and walked past her, my hand up as if to lead the way.

"Let's meet in the conference room."

I didn't want her inside my office. I didn't need the scent of her perfume lingering or any of that magic weaseling her way into me long after she was gone. On my way over, I composed myself. This project was important; this project was for both Sam and me. Inside the conference room, everything was set up. I idled around the seat at the head of the table, my normal seat. It felt presumptuous to take the spot with Tessa here. A part of me wanted to offer it to her. I shook the thought away. Kid. Boyfriend. I took a seat across from where she stood. She was talking quietly to Chloe, who was swiping that digital clipboard as Sam took a seat to my right. Tessa kicked off the meeting by describing the four projects we were providing fabrics for. She went on to explain some ideas they'd come up with. What she knew was the fabrics that would work, and that was enough for me since it was the only thing I needed to know. Unfortunately, the fabric that stood out most was one of the ones the Colombian women had and refused to sell me. I wouldn't bring that up yet. I'd work on it in private, and when I knew it was something I could bring to the table, I'd offer it. In the meantime, we'd have to go in a different direction. I could tell she knew what she wanted to do for the Spring Collection and the hotel, but the car seemed to be eating at her.

"Do you have a concept for it?" I asked once Tessa was finished speaking.

"No." Her jaw clenched when she said it.

I bit back a smile. She was mad about this. I stood and walked over to her, not missing the way she took a step back and her eyes widened the way they always did when she thought I was going to do something crazy. My heart did a little skip. She was standing directly in front of the blueprint of the interior of the hotel and didn't move when I stood beside her and my arm brushed against hers. I wondered if she felt the spark.

There was no way she didn't feel the spark.

I splayed my hand on the paper and scanned it as if I had anything to do with the actual design or concept, which I didn't.

"It's a nice space to work with."

"It is," she agreed with a little shaky laugh that made me smile. She reached her hand out and Chloe handed her clipboard over. It was nice to see she still had the gift of not saying a word and having people know exactly what she needed. She clicked a tab and pulled up a picture of the first project she reviewed with us, the car.

"How do you like working with Ryan?"

Her gaze snapped to mine. "You know him."

"You can say that."

I'd met Ryan while my father was still the head of Hawthorne and our business relationship had only gotten stronger after I took over. He was always very professional and had exceptional instincts when it came to business. The man also had a different woman at his side every time I saw him. I wasn't sure that I liked knowing he was working closely with Tessa. *Kid.* I reminded myself. *Possible boyfriend.* I fought an annoyed groan and looked at her left hand. She had no ring on it, so either the boyfriend had become an ex or he still hadn't asked her to marry him, in which case, he was a fucking moron. Hypocrisy at its best. I knew it, but I owned it.

"I haven't met him yet," she said. "He's been on vacation all week."

"Did you get here this week?"

"No." She blinked away from me. Briefly looked at the clipboard in her hand and then back up at me. "I started working this week. We all did."

Sam cleared his throat from the other side of the room. I glanced up at him. He raised an eyebrow as if to ask me what the fuck I was doing.

The project.

Right.

"You'll have to let me know what your concept is so we can narrow down fabrics, unless you already have exactly what you want in mind. Colors, materials, etcetera."

Tessa handed Chloe back the clipboard and picked up her phone to look at the time. In the two-seconds she had it lit up, I caught sight of a little boy smiling at the camera. He had the bluest blue eyes I'd ever seen. My heart slammed hard in my chest. She had a boy. I glanced away quickly.

"I have to go," she said quickly.

"We haven't even discussed fabrics," I argued.

She exhaled, bringing her hands up and rubbing her temple with the tips of her fingers. When she dropped them again, she looked at Chloe. "I need you to—"

"I got it." Chloe stood and grabbed her things before giving my brother a quick hug. Watching them together was almost painful. It reminded me of what I didn't have and seemed to crave these days. Who would have ever imagined that?

"Thank you," Tessa called out as Chloe walked out of the room. Chloe flashed her a smile.

"I should stay, right?" Seth asked.

"No. Go back to Prim and work with Tommy to finish the designs." Tessa exhaled and looked over at me. "Do you have fabrics here? Swatches of colors? Anything?"

"Yes, to both."

"I'll need to see them." She looked back at Seth. "I'll see you Monday. Meeting at ten. Don't forget. Once that's done, we'll meet and discuss. Hopefully by then, one of us will have come up with something."

Seth stood, did a little salute, and walked out.

"And then there were three," Sam said, smiling.

Tessa smiled. I felt myself smile as well. It felt both foreign and familiar, and not for the first time since she walked into the building, I wondered how I'd ever let this woman go. If I were to rewind, I wouldn't take any of it back, especially not after seeing how all of this had affected the unbreakable Camryn. If it had been Tessa in her place, I would have alienated her. Not purposely, but it would have happened. She had a demanding career and I'd wanted more out of mine. Things would never have worked between us and I wouldn't have been able to live with myself if I'd purposely pushed her away. Looking at how guarded she seemed around me, I guess I ended up doing it anyway.

We sat and focused on the fabrics, textures, and different colors. She seemed to hate everything I showed her. When Tessa pulled the third fabric book toward her, Sam stood and stretched.

"I need to get going. If the furniture company doesn't get the fabrics delivered by Saturday, this guy's gonna have our heads." His gaze turned to Tessa. "You good? Do you need me to—"

"Nope. It's taken care of. Thanks."

They were finishing each other's sentences and even though I knew it was stupid to let it bother me, it did. They'd stayed in touch these years while I'd disappeared and I knew he had a relationship with her son even if he never actually talked about the little boy. He'd also never spoken to me about the kid's dad. I'd found out enough information about the guy to appease my curiosity and retracted before I went any further. It wouldn't have been fair to either of us. But now that she was here? I'd have to keep myself in check. I wouldn't be the Mariah in this situation, pulling her away from her boyfriend.

CHAPTER TEN

TESSA

I FELT JITTERY AROUND HIM. I couldn't help it. The combination of nerves and guilt made up one hell of a concoction swishing inside me, making me feel tipsy with emotion. I glanced up and found him watching me closely.

"Have you looked at the sketches of the socks?"

"Briefly," I said. "I've been a little more focused on the bigger contracts." I met his gaze. "No offense."

"None taken."

"Why socks?"

"Well, we all wear them, for one," he said, a hint of a smile tugging his lips. "Besides that, I wanted to have something that's mine."

"Hawthorne Industries isn't yours?" I raised an eyebrow.

"Something that I started, that I built."

I felt myself nod in understanding. "What's RHS Designs?"

"Rowan, Hawthorne, Samson," he said.

"Oh. Wow. Sam didn't tell me about that."

"It's fairly new. I wanted to rebrand." He turned around and leaned against the conference table. He was standing right by me. If I moved my hand a little too far to the left, it would touch his. I reckon he knew that, probably did it on purpose and relished the sense of imbalance I felt at his nearness. He inched closer still. I set my pencil down, leaned back in my seat, and crossed my arms. When I looked over to him, my heartbeat doubled when our gazes met, which I hated.

"What's your deal?"

"What deal?" He crossed his arms, cocked his head, and stared at me.

"Why are you looking at me like that? Sitting so close?"

"I can't look at you?"

"Not like that."

"I only know how to look at you one way."

I swallowed the question, afraid to ask what way he meant even though I already knew. He was making me imagine things that scared me all over again. "I can't do my job if you keep at it."

"I'm not doing anything." His eyes glittered. I could tell he was holding back a smile.

"Rowan, I know you," I said. "Did you forget? I know you better than most."

"You know me better than all."

There went my galloping heart again, running off with ideas. I tried to school my features as best as I could. I should tell him about Miles, but I didn't know what to say, how to start. "Hey, by the way, we have a son. Sorry it took me almost four years to tell you," wasn't nearly good enough.

No. I couldn't just blurt it out. I'd take this weekend to think and tell him on Monday. I took a deep breath, let it out, and smiled.

"Let's get back to work."

He stared at me for a moment longer before giving a nod and launching into an explanation about the socks.

"You don't even have a cute logo for these?" I asked.

"Not yet."

"But—" I blinked from him to the sock sketches and back to him. "Who sketched these?"

"Sam."

I looked at the socks again. They weren't bad, per se, they just weren't clean. He'd done them on the computer instead of by hand. Call me a purist, but I wasn't a fan of computer programs drawing for me. "Really?"

"Can you help me?"

"You hired us, didn't you?"

"Yes, but I don't want Seth or someone else in your department. I want you."

The words curled inside me, my body clearly taking that as a double entendre, which it surely wasn't, but this was Rowan and every single thing that slipped out of those full lips had a purpose. I must have stayed quiet too long, because he bumped his chair to mine. "Tessa," he whispered.

"No." I kept my eyes fixed on the sketch in front of me. "We aren't doing this again, Rowan. We aren't. We work, we talk about work, and that's it."

He shifted and finally took the seat next to mine. "Have you forgiven me? Just answer me that."

"I'm over it. That's the only thing you need to know right now."

Our conversation was cut short by Samson coming back into the conference room. He looked at us. "You guys are still here?"

"Yeah." I pushed the side button on my phone and looked at the time. I was going to miss dinner. "Shit." I stood, gathering my things. "I have to go. Are you free tomorrow morning?" I looked at Rowan. He nodded, eyes unwavering on mine. Those eyes always got me, damn it. I left before I could say anything. Samson caught up to me.

"You didn't tell him." It wasn't a question. I pushed the elevator button.

"Not yet. Give me this weekend, Sam. I can't just spring that on him. I have so much shit resting on my shoulders right now."

"I'll give you the weekend," he said. "I won't keep it from him any longer than that."

"You really didn't know? Every time you looked at Miles, you really didn't have a clue?" I knew I'd struck a nerve at the way his eyes widened slightly. I stepped into the elevator. "That's what I thought. You've kept it for over three years."

"I didn't know."

"He looks exactly like him," I said. "Maybe you didn't want to believe it or see it, but you must have suspected."

He pursed his lips. "I didn't know."

"We'll go with that, but don't you dare tell him. I'm not kidding. I have my reasons for not telling him yet."

"Because you're holding a grudge."

"Please, Sam. I'm not a child," I said, jabbing the button so that the doors wouldn't close between us. "This is much more than a grudge and you know it."

I went home. Thankfully, Celia had already taken care of bath time and had Miles in his astronaut pajamas. His dark hair had already been brushed to the side and he had a goofy smile on his face when I walked in.

"Mommy!"

"Hey, baby, I'm so sorry I'm late," I said, crouching and wrapping my arms around him so I could inhale the scent of his jasmine baby wash. I thought about my meeting with Rowan and the way Sam was insisting I tell him everything. Without so much as a hint of warning, emotion surged inside me, and I started to weep against him. He was my baby, my everything. He'd been with me when I was pregnant and scared and when I didn't know what the hell I was doing once he was born. I'd woken up every hour, on the hour, to feed him. I was the one who had lain awake with him on my chest when he got his first fever. Sure, I had help from my sister and grandmother, but he was my son. What was I supposed to do when Rowan demanded weekends with him? Just let him go? My sister sighed heavily from the kitchen.

"I'll be right back."

I glanced up at her and nodded, smiling. "Thank you."

"Always, babe."

Once she walked out, I looked at Miles. "Did you have a good day at daycare today?"

He nodded, smiling. "Made a tree with no leaves for fall."

"That sounds fun. What else?"

"Drew a rocket."

"That's exciting." I smiled and lifted him higher in my arms. "Was it blue?"

"Blue and white."

"Ooohh, blue and white. Impressive."

I carried him to the bathroom and set him down in front of the sink. He went over to the toilet. I smiled as he went about his business, aiming into the toilet as if there were imaginary Cheerios there. That was how I potty trained him—Cheerios in the toilet. He flushed and came over to the sink, stepping onto the little stool. I thought about Samson as I watched Miles wash his hands. He had looked so utterly betrayed he when I admitted that Rowan was Miles's father. Deep down, I knew he'd always suspected it, but like a true friend, he hadn't pushed me, and like an awful friend, I hadn't come clean about it. Looking back, I'd had plenty of opportunities, but Sam had been sick and I'd been busy with work and Miles. It wasn't as if all of us were sitting around lounging while I was keeping this lie and it wasn't as if Sam was the only person I'd kept the truth from. The only people who knew were Celia and Grandma Joan. Everyone else was in the dark. It was easier that way.

Miles dried his hands and lifted his arms up for me to carry him again, the way he often did when it was his bedtime and I hadn't seen him all day. His tiny arms wrapped tightly around my neck as I carried him into his room, only loosening when I settled him into bed.

"Story?" he asked over a yawn. I pushed his hair back.

"Not today, baby. You're tired. I'm tired. We'll read two stories tomorrow."

"Kay," he whispered, his eyes drifting shut. I kissed both his cheeks and whispered good night.

My sister was walking back in when I stepped into the kitchen area.

"Are you okay?" she asked, her brows pulling in.

The wave of emotion I'd been holding in suddenly came crashing down. I shook my head rapidly, trying to hold in the tears and failing. "I'm not."

I recounted everything that happened. She hugged me tighter with each word I spoke and held my head against her chest as I cried afterward.

"Just take the weekend to think about it," she said. "Maybe it's time."

"I have to go back to his office tomorrow."

"So, you go back there, act natural, get through Friday, and start over on Monday. Maybe this is a blessing in disguise. Stop worrying."

I vowed to try.

———————

IT WAS casual Friday and I took full advantage of it, wearing jeans, a nice black-and-white blouse with a pretty ribbon in the neck, and black converse. I looped my messenger bag over my shoulder. The subway ride was eventful, as most subway rides were if you were actually paying attention, which I was because I'd stuffed my phone in my bag first and I had no interest in rubbing elbows with the person beside me to get it out. Not that I had much room for elbow rubbing to begin with. I was glad when my stop arrived.

I'd spent the entire night tossing and turning and rehearsing how I would tell him we had a son together. Then I spent my morning rehearsing how I would tell Miles about his father. It wasn't that Miles had never asked, but I'd always left things unanswered. I'd just shifted the conversation to the many wonderful father figures he had—Freddie, Samson, and my dad.

How many times had I dreamed of telling him when Miles was a baby? I'd stopped once Miles started to sleep through the night and no longer felt like I was losing my mind all the time. And yet, there I was, about to be face to face with the guy, and I had absolutely no inclination to tell him. No urge to scream, *"We have a son together,"* at the top of my lungs. Nothing. Maybe it was because I had so much help and my life had started coming together without a man in my life.

Maybe it was self-preservation.

Regardless, I pulled the door open and went up to the fifth floor. Each step I took was filled with a nervous tension. Even small talk with Sam, who met me in the lobby, didn't seem to help. He seemed to notice, because as we were nearing Rowan's office, he stopped walking, put his hand on my shoulder, and made me look at him.

"I'm sorry about yesterday," he said. "You okay?"

"I'm sorry too and I'm fine. Promise." I offered him a little smile.

"You wear your emotions on your sleeve."

"I know." I also knew Rowan could read me like the back of his hand and would read whatever was showing on my face. I took a breath and tried for serious. "How 'bout now?"

"'Cause I'm up right now," Sam sang-slash-rapped.

"And you suck right now," I finished.

We were still laughing when Rowan's door opened. He stood there, his blue eyes bouncing between us, and shook his head. That was different from how it had been before. He used to look at us with a hint of contempt. I wasn't sure if everything Sam had been through was the cause of this newfound good mood when it came to our friendship or maybe he'd found enough happiness in his personal life—with Camryn—to care.

I looked at Sam again. "Thanks."

"Always." He winked before tossing out a, "Let me know if you need anything," and walking away.

I faced Rowan. I had no choice but to. He held the door open for me, his mouth twitching as I brushed past him. "Converse. There's the girl I know."

"Casual Friday." I eyed him in his navy suit. "You should try it sometime."

He smiled that warm smile that made me feel things I shouldn't. It reminded me of his son, who was in daycare waiting for Celia to pick him up with a snack and a drink in her hands. My mom and grandmother would be here this evening, and that meant a late night for all of us while they drank their wine and adjusted to the time difference. I went over to the table he had set up off to the side, similar to my own office layout. I said as much.

"Is it nice?" he asked. "Your office."

"Very."

I glanced outside at the view his office had. It was on a much lower floor than mine, so I couldn't see much of the city, but it felt cozy. It felt like home. I blinked away from the view before I could delve into that thought. It only felt cozy because it was Brooklyn. I sat in one of the chairs and tapped the armrest.

"Fancy," I said, wondering how much he'd spent on it. Probably as much as I was paying for Mile's daycare.

You wanted that, I reminded myself. *You wanted to do it on your own. You didn't want his mother or Camryn meddling or having any part in your son's life. You made that choice.*

"It would probably look better in your office."

"You've never seen it."

"Not yet, but I know enough about Ryan to know he wouldn't leave Harold unless he was going to be making bank and working somewhere even fancier," he said. "Maybe we can meet there next time."

"Or you can go meet your buddy Ryan." Whom I still hadn't even met. I added that part under my breath. Rowan chuckled.

"He's a strange one."

"Is he?" I gave him my full attention, figuring he was about to give me the scoop on my new co-worker.

"He has a lot of connections." He paused. "Let's just say he doesn't have to work; he chooses to."

"Trust fund baby? He seems like he would be."

"Exactly." He grinned. I looked away. I didn't need that grin in my life. The replica I had at home was much sweeter.

I waved my hand over the board. "Show me the magic."

He seemed to stall for a second too long. I looked over at him and caught him staring. My pulse spiked.

"What?"

"Nothing." He blinked, clearing his throat.

I forced my eyes back to the board. I seriously needed not to do this. It wasn't that I hadn't connected with other people after him. There was Cody, of course, but I didn't want to ruin our friendship. There had been French Dude, which was what Celia and I called him. He'd been smart and good-looking and attentive as hell, but I had Miles, and he trumped everyone. French Dude tried to be all cool and nonchalant, but deep down, he was needy. Or maybe he was just needy about sex and cuddling—two things I couldn't give him as often as all the other single girls in the city of lights could.

The digital board powered up and showed me all sorts of fabric colors. Fiery reds and vibrant blues. Rowan taught me how to scroll and search. I touched an ivory and a blue I kept going back to. He jotted down the numbers and clicked on a different little device to see if they had them in this location.

"How many locations are you up to now?"

"Three, but this is the main one. We still have the one back home, but it's been turned into a factory. London is still there because of Mom, but we had to let go of a lot of employees and downsized. I'm working on Colombia and Guatemala. I hit a roadblock there."

"You? I didn't think you knew what a roadblock was." My god, he was definitely sitting too close to me. I adjusted my seat, rolled it an inch away.

"It's boring stuff." He waved a hand. "I'm sure you don't want to hear about it."

"I do want to hear about it, actually, but I can't right now."

"Got somewhere to be?"

I took out my phone and looked at the screen. No missed calls. No texts. Miles would be out of daycare in a few minutes, though, and I wanted to get home before Mom and Grandma

Joan did to make sure everything was picked up so neither one of them bitched about the mess. As if living with a toddler was anything but messy. I pushed the side button and looked up at him.

"My mom and Joan are coming in today," I said. "I need to pick up the apartment before they get there and start judging."

"I'm sure they'll forgive you."

I cracked my neck as he stood and pulled out three massive leather books from a shelf. I'd know those books anywhere. They were filled with fabric swatches, which made my heart pitter-patter a little. At Prim, I'd been stuck in the design room for over a year, and sadly, Yamina was the one who was sorting through the fabric for all of the designs. The magnitude of these projects finally hit me as Rowan set those massive books down in front of me. These were my projects. Mine to oversee and take responsibility for.

"You look like you're about to cry." His voice sounded funny. I looked up and found him watching me with an unreadable expression on his face. "Is it me?"

"No. Sorry." I blinked rapidly. "It's the fabric."

"Oh."

All his disappointment was wrapped up in that one little word. The one he said all clipped and final when he didn't get the answer he was expecting.

"You can take them home," he said, clearing his throat.

"The books?"

"Yeah." He came around and sat beside me again. He looked so weird with that beard. It wasn't as if it was a super big lumber-jack beard, but still. A beard was a beard and seeing one on Rowan was . . . weird. And hot . . . "Take all of them if you want. It's Friday. I'm the only one who gets the urge to look through these on the weekend anyway."

Hm. "I bet your wife loves that."

I cringed inwardly. I hadn't exactly meant to say that aloud or for the statement to come out so snappy. It made it sound like I potentially cared about that whole thing when, in reality, I didn't. But if I was even going to consider telling Rowan about Miles, I needed to know I'd be doing the right thing and that Camryn wouldn't be an issue.

"I'm getting a divorce." The words tumbled out of his mouth. My eyes snapped to his before dropping to his left hand, which was ring-less. "And I'm in the process of buying the company from my grandparents."

"Oh. Good. That's . . . great news. I know how much you wanted this." I gave him a polite smile.

A few years ago, I would have killed to hear those words. Right then? I didn't care about him or his company or his wife or his lack of a wedding ring. The only thing I cared about was Miles and how this would affect him if—huge if—I let Rowan into his life.

"Anyway," I said, needing to say something because he was giving me the look he gave when he couldn't believe my reaction to something. "I wouldn't be able to carry all of these."

"I can help." He glanced at his watch. "I'm calling it a day anyway."

"No, I'll just take—"

"Just let me help. Are you going back to the office or home?"

"Home."

"Where's home?"

"Not far from here."

He raised an eyebrow. "You live in Brooklyn? When did that happen?"

"When I moved back." I still hadn't given him specifics about that and I couldn't imagine why he kept fishing.

"In that case, I'll definitely help you."

I eyed the books. The darn things probably weighed more

than Miles. My little man was scrawny and always shimmying here and there so it was impossible for him to put weight on. He was a big boy and wanted to do big boy things. I smiled.

"I'd kill to know what put that smile on your face," Rowan said, his voice low.

"Just business." I made sure to keep my voice businesslike.

Maybe I was warning myself because with the way my heart doubled in speed, I was obviously the one who needed the reminder. A month ago, I would have sworn on a stack of bibles that I was over him but having him in front of me and feeling like this had me second-guessing that.

"Thank you." I tried to grab one of the books, but he didn't let me, insisting he carry all three.

I didn't argue.

We only had three blocks to walk, which was a bit disconcerting, but he didn't comment. In fact, we walked mostly in silence. When we stopped to wait for the walk light to blink, he nodded in the direction of the street we were on.

"My place is right up there."

"Oh." I followed his gaze, heart thumping. He literally lived one block away from me. The light turned and we made our way across the street. Every step I took felt like the decision was being made for me. I should tell him about Miles. He didn't deserve that gift, but my little boy did, and despite any thought and grudge I may hold against Rowan, I knew he was a good man. A loving man. I blinked rapidly.

"This is me," I said, coming to a stop in front of my building.

"You're joking."

"Not joking." I let out a nervous laugh, holding my arms out to take the books.

"You aren't inviting me up?" He seemed surprised by this.

"Definitely not."

"I suppose your boyfriend wouldn't approve." I was about to

ask him what boyfriend he was talking about, but he shifted, placing the books carefully into my arms. I grunted a little. He had carried them so effortlessly that I had almost expected them not to be as heavy as I thought they were. "I wouldn't approve either."

"Why? You're just helping me carry some books."

"Only a fool with think that."

"Hold the door." My brother's voice snapped my attention behind Rowan. Freddie looked from me to Rowan and then back to me with that unreadable expression of his.

"Ro," he said.

"Long time no see." Rowan smiled as he gave my brother one of those pat, sideways hugs. "You haven't changed a bit."

Freddie slapped him on the shoulder, grinning. "How's New York treating you?

"Fine, though I gotta say that not having the water right behind me every day is killing me."

"I bet. I'm surprised you can survive without it."

"It's all I've been doing these past years." Rowan dragged his gaze back to me. "Merely surviving."

I rolled my eyes and handed the books over to Freddie. "Carry these for me, please. I have to head up." I smiled sweetly and blew him a kiss before turning to Rowan. "See you . . . I guess I'll have to get the books back to you Monday, so I'll have Sam pick them up."

"I can pick them up."

"Sure." I turned and opened the door. "Have a good weekend."

I walked to the elevator and looked outside to where my brother and Rowan were still talking. I was so grateful to be out of Rowan's presence. I was sure they'd talk about working out, Hawthorne Industries, or The Company, which Freddie refused to talk about to Celia and I, but I would bet money he'd talk about it with Rowan. I had my key in my hand, ready to unlock my door, when Celia opened it. I paused.

"Where's Miles?"

"Napping."

"Oh." I frowned, dropping my messenger bag by the door and then kicking my heels off. "Where were you going?"

"Nowhere. I heard the elevator ding and knew it was you." She went around to the kitchen and got a glass of water. "Want coffee?"

"No." I took a seat on the stool. "I'll take a bottle of water."

"Freddie called saying he was on his way too. I ordered Chinese."

"That sounds so good right now." My stomach growled as she handed me the water. "He's downstairs."

"Why didn't he come up with you?"

I opened the water bottle and started chugging it. When I put it down, she was still watching me curiously. "He's talking to Rowan."

"What?" Her eyes widened. "What's he doing here?"

"We had a meeting today and he offered to let me borrow some fabric books. He carried them over for me."

"He isn't coming up, is he?"

"No." I heaved a tired sigh. "It's bad enough that I can't think straight when he's around, there is no way I'm inviting that man into my home."

When I finished, her mouth was hanging open. The list of things that made my sister lose her words had just expanded to include my admitting I wasn't quite immune to my ex-boyfriend and father of my baby coming back into my life. She blinked and then looked in the direction of Miles's bedroom.

"What does this mean for him?"

"Nothing," I said. She raised her eyebrows and I added, "Nothing yet."

"Is he still with the bitch?"

"He mentioned a divorce, but that means she's still in the picture in some capacity."

"Well, Sam is going to tell him if you don't," Celia offered.

"I know," I said. "I just . . . I'm scared. I'm scared about having Camryn or Mildred around him when I'm not present."

My heart hurt just thinking about it. What if Camryn gave him Benadryl to make him shut up and go to sleep? A cold shudder ran through me.

"No. I can't just tell him. I need to be sure of so many things before that is even a possibility," I said, and Celia nodded sadly, reaching over and placing her warm hand on mine.

"I get it," she whispered. "I really do, but he deserves to know his son, and Miles deserves to know his father."

The ache in my chest worsened. I knew she was right, but I wasn't ready yet. Not yet.

CHAPTER ELEVEN

TESSA

I HELD my drink a little tighter as I looked at Celia from across the bar slash lounge slash restaurant that Sam's friend owned. She ran into some editor from her publishing house and had been talking to him since we got here. Before walking off to continue her conversation, she handed me a bourbon concoction and told me to approach a man I was attracted to and flirt with him.

"That's step one," she'd said. *"I'm sure you know where the rest leads."*

Find a man I was attracted to and flirt with him. If it wasn't for Celia pushing me to do this, I would've gladly stayed home.

Still. It seemed simple enough. I scanned the bar, feeling flutters in my stomach. There were a ton of good-looking guys, but I couldn't just go up to one. Could I? One guy across the bar met my gaze and I stiffened, bringing the tiny straw up to my lips and glancing away quickly but not quickly enough. He was making his way over and I took a step back, looking up with a smile when he neared. Oh my god. Why did I ever look around? It was Cody, and he looked non-too-happy to see me here.

"You look like you're trying to disappear into the topiary," he said.

I smiled. "I was going to call you. I swear."

"Why didn't you?"

"I started working and between that and Miles, things haven't exactly been . . . smooth."

"Yet, here you are, having a drink at a bar like a grown-up."

"Would you believe me I told you Celia made me do it?"

He titled his head and shook it slightly before letting out a bark of laughter. "Actually, I would. I'm glad you're here."

I kind of pushed myself into his hug, holding my drink away from us. When I pulled back, he eyed it.

"What are you drinking?"

"I'm not really sure. It has a lot of bourbon and a little bit of something else I can't quite place because, well, the bourbon."

He chuckled, clinking his glass against mine just as Sam and Chloe sidled up next to us. "Hi, Cody!" Chloe gave him a side hug as Sam shot me a questioning look. I just shrugged, not knowing how to explain Cody being at the grand opening.

The longer I stood there, the more fucked up I felt, and not just with my drink. It was messed up that I didn't call Cody when I got Stateside when he'd called me every time he landed in a city he knew I'd be in for a convention.

"You want to join us for dinner?" Chloe asked.

Cody looked at me, as if waiting for an answer.

I smiled. "Why not?"

"Sure."

On our walk over, I stopped and told Celia I was going next door for dinner and asked her to join us.

"I'll pass but come back when you're done. I'll be here." She said hi to Cody, who was behind me and looked at me again, saying everything she could possibly say with those expressive eyes of hers. I shot her a warning glance.

"Sam, buy her another drink," Celia said.

"I'm on it," Sam said behind me.

"I got it," Chloe added, wiggling one of the glasses in her hand before handing it over. "This one's yours."

We sat in a large booth—Sam and Chloe beside each other, Cody and I across from them. I took a sip of the drink Chloe had given me and eyed the menu.

"I'm not really hungry and don't want to lose my buzz, so I am just going to sit and drink while I wait for dessert."

"I think I'll do the same," Chloe announced.

"I guess I'll stay sober," Sam said.

"How's Miles handling being in the states?" Cody asked.

"He loves it. He's still in daycare. Full day."

"He can probably teach his peers a thing or two. Kid started reading when he was two years old," Sam said, interrupting. "He talks about things I didn't even know kids knew about."

"That's impressive."

"He's the cutest," Chloe added.

"Are you talking about me again, Chloe?"

I nearly jumped out of my skin at his voice and then shot Sam a glare for not warning me that Rowan would be here.

"Not talking about you." Chloe smiled and shook her head.

"I thought you said you weren't coming," Sam said.

"You aren't glad I'm here?"

Cody's phone started to vibrate on the table and he glanced

at the screen before giving me an apologetic look. "I'll be right back."

I sighed, watching him walk off. Rowan took the opportunity to slide into the booth beside me, so close I could smell his cologne. I wanted to rip it off him and stomp on it and all of the memories it brought back.

"I didn't want to miss the grand opening. It looks nice, Sam. Really nice." He looked around for good measure. I took a healthy gulp of my drink, which was completely going straight to my head.

"I am such a bitch," I said.

Sam cleared his throat and made a show of picking up the menu. "Maybe we should order you some food."

"Leave her alone. She's getting laid tonight. She's allowed to loosen up," Chloe said.

I felt Rowan stiffen beside me. Was it me or was he seriously too close to me? I started to feel hot and pressed closer to the inside of the booth, taking another sip before Sam lifted the glass from my hand and set it on his side of the table.

"Hey!"

"Nope. You shouldn't be going home with anyone if you're tipsy," Sam commented.

"What if it's Cody?" Chloe asked in a mock whisper.

"Especially not if it's Cody." I frowned. "I'm not trying to ruin a friendship. I was supposed to click with some random guy and fuck him. One-night stand, you know?"

Rowan exhaled heavily beside me. He waved down the waitress and ordered himself a scotch, neat.

"He's cute though, right?" I looked at Chloe. She nodded, eyes wide.

"Make it a double please," Rowan told the waitress. "And bring two."

I glanced over to him. He looked so fucking good. He smelled so fucking good too. I may have said that aloud, because his eyes sparkled. Maybe he read my mind. Either way, I added, "I hate you."

"That makes two of us," he replied.

"Maybe Ro and I should go talk to some people while you guys eat," Sam said.

"So, this guy Cody is just your friend?" Rowan asked casually, completely ignoring his brother. "Not your boyfriend?"

"Boyfriend?" Chloe scoffed. "Do you know her?"

Rowan's eyes were smoldering when they met mine. "Oh, I know her."

"Rowan." My voice may have sounded a little breathless and a lot needy. His eyes darkened even more. He put his hand beside mine on the booth, his fingertips touching mine, my pulse jumping with the simple move. I couldn't make myself look away, not even as Chloe continued talking about my and Cody's friendship. Somehow, Rowan's hand ended up over mine completely, his eyes on me as if he were afraid to look anywhere else. With each passing second, I felt my breath slip away a little more.

"Don't go home with him," he whispered.

"You have no right to ask that of me," I whispered back.

"I know I don't, and that fucking kills me, but please, don't go home with him."

"If I asked you not to go home to your wife, would you listen?" I needed to break this spell, but I couldn't seem to gather the strength to actually do it, a shortcoming I blamed on the bourbon. Definitely.

"Stop calling her my wife," he said.

"Isn't that what she is?"

"On paper."

"Isn't that all a marriage is? A piece of paper?"

"Tessa." It was a groan, a plea. I moved my hand from underneath his and put it on my lap, he reached over and grabbed it again, threading his fingers through mine. "It's a sham, and you know it." It was the caress of his thumb across the sensitive skin of my wrist that made heat pool between my legs. I gripped his hand tighter in warning. He looked like he was having a hard time not touching me.

Cody walked back to the table and I forced myself to tear my gaze away from Rowan and sit upright.

"I think I may try Tessa's diet tonight," Cody said.

"Cody, tell Sam we've never slept together." Cody chuckled, but his eyes held no amusement. Rowan's hand tightened around mine beneath the table.

"We haven't," he said and then looked at Rowan. "Nice to see you again."

"Likewise," Rowan responded in a voice that sounded anything but pleasant.

Sam put his menu down again. "Ro, let's go talk to—"

"No, I'm perfectly fine right here," Rowan said, interrupting Sam. The waitress brought his drinks and set them in front of him before asking if we were ready to order. Sam ordered three appetizers for the table and shot me a warning look as I grabbed my drink back.

"You're so bossy today." I giggled. Fucking giggled, and I didn't even care that I sounded like a child. I felt good. I felt free. I hadn't experienced the New York nightlife and if this was it, I was totally about it. I mean, as long as Miles was home sleeping it wasn't as if I was missing out on anything. Not even Rowan could dampen my mood.

"Have you taken Miles anywhere fun?" Cody asked.

"Not yet. I'm telling you, we haven't had time."

"Miles?" Rowan asked. His grip tightened. Our gazes clashed and I swore my whole world pitched on its axis.

Cody's phone buzzed again. He exhaled loudly. "Sorry. Be right back."

"Tessa, why don't you and Rowan switch seats?" Sam suggested, clearly trying to save me. "So, you won't have to speak over the table?"

"Good idea." I tried to take my hand back from Rowan's.

"Absolutely not."

"What? Why not?" I pulled my hand again.

"Because I'm comfortable here."

"That's a stupid reason." I raised an eyebrow, shook my hand in his once more. Finally, he let go, but he didn't move.

"You want me to switch seats so you can flirt? No."

His words hit me quick and hard. I blinked. Even in my tipsy state I could tell that he was jealous. *Jealous!* For some reason, I found it both humorous and offensive.

"You got married," I said in what I thought was a hushed whisper but probably wasn't. "Seriously. Switch seats."

"Ro, switch seats with her." Sam's voice was almost a plea.

"This is unbelievable." Rowan slid out of the booth and I followed, taking a deep breath when I stood. He caught my elbow, those blue eyes intense on mine, and leaned in. "For the record, I don't like seeing you flirt with other men."

"For the record, I don't like seeing you married to other women." I yanked my elbow away.

He glowered at me another beat before sliding into the booth. I slid in after, staying closer to Cody's side. When he walked back toward the booth, he smiled wide.

"I like this seating arrangement," he announced, sliding in beside me and leaning close to whisper, "You okay with you-know-who? What's the deal with that situation?"

"Nothing. There is no deal." I tried—and failed—to laugh it off. "No deal. Get it?" I was looking at Rowan, who was watching me like he wanted to flip this table over and kill someone. It made me smile wider. I definitely needed to drink more water. I pulled a glass to me.

Sam cleared his throat from the other side of the table just as my phone vibrated in my purse. A text message alert. I fished it out and looked at it.

Sam: You need to tell him. You just said Miles's name.

I rolled my eyes, but my heart did a little thrash as I typed out a quick response.

Me: I need time.

Sam: He isn't an idiot.

Me: You knew I named him Miles, you've seen him a million times, and you still say you didn't know.

I glanced up at Sam. His eyes met mine, narrowing in warning. My phone buzzed again.

Sam: Stop talking to Cody about Miles in front of him. It's fucked up.

Me: I'm fucked up.

Sam: Trust me, we all know that. Stop drinking if you're really going home with him. PS. I don't think you should.

Me: Thanks, Dad.

Sam: Trying to look out for you.

That made my frown deepen. Cody spoke and took my attention off the situation, but my mind stayed on Sam and the texts and Rowan, who I couldn't seem to get away from no matter where I went. Whose face I saw every time I looked at the little boy who owned my heart.

CHAPTER TWELVE

ROWAN

I WATCHED Tessa and Cody sort of dance as they flirted and knew this was what hell must have felt like. Then I reminded myself of the time I saw her when she was pregnant and had been beautiful and glowing and laughing with this very man. She said she had never slept with him, which would mean the boy wasn't his, but evidentially, she was into one-night stands. Fuck. I'd give my left arm to have one of those with her.

Who the fuck put that baby inside her and left?

Maybe he hadn't left, maybe she was the one who walked away.

Oh, God. What if she was raped? I shut that thought down. It was too inconceivable to even consider.

I shouldn't have been pondering any of this in the first place. It was clear she was over me. Sure, she may still find me attractive. Sure, there was still that invisible line between us that seemed to vibrate whenever she was near, but none of those things mattered. Not even love seemed to matter. She'd told me she loved me, and I'd turned her away. I didn't deserve any more than this.

"You look miserable."

I turned to see my friend Dean beside me. "The way you walk through crowds and go unnoticed is scary."

"Part of my charm." His mouth tilted up slightly.

He wasn't a huge guy. At first sight, I would've bet money I could take him down, but he had this glint in his eyes that instilled fear in those around him. I was sure he'd won plenty of fights with that glint alone. I'd met Dean at a bar not long after I'd seen Tessa pregnant at that convention. Needless to say, I was alone and drunk as hell. We sparked up a conversation, mostly me rambling on and on about it, and he said he'd do me a once in a lifetime favor and find out everything about the guy she was with. I'd laughed it off but had given him my phone number nonetheless. With not much to go on, he'd found Cody Maverick. That was when I figured out where we'd met. Jealousy had torn through me, but knowing they'd met because of me really kicked my ass. Dean and I became fast friends afterward, even though he wasn't very forthcoming with his information. He was always out of town working, but I didn't have a clue what he did for work or whether or not he had a family. I didn't know much about him at all, except that he was loyal and kind underneath his rugged exterior. I glanced at him.

"I'm surprised you're in town."

"Work."

"Hm." I commented. "Stalking people?"

His lips twitched ever so slightly. "You could say that."

I shook my head and turned my attention back to Tessa and Cody. I wanted nothing more than to rip his hand off the spot on her waist. She seemed comfortable around him and completely okay with his advances. She seemed so happy and free around him and so guarded around me. I hated the thought of that, but I couldn't blame her.

"That's your chick, isn't it?" Dean asked. I blinked over to him.

"If she were my chick . . ." I said, chuckling around the word. I would love to see Tessa's face if I ever referred to her as my chick. "That guy would have no fingers when I was done with him."

This made Dean laugh wholeheartedly. "I'd actually pay to see that."

"I guess she's back in town for good," I said.

"With Cody Maverick in tow."

"I'm surprised you remember his name." It'd been a long time ago.

"I remember everything. All the time."

"Some would say it's a gift."

"Some," he agreed, meeting my gaze again. "Would you?"

Somehow, I felt he knew the answer to that. I looked at Tessa again, thinking about all the things I remembered and would love to forget. Even if I did try to get her back, there were too many things in our way. The contracts for the company were still pending, probably sitting on the desk of my grandfather's lawyer. My divorce was pending, still sitting on Camryn's lap while she doodled on the pages with her stupid pink pen as if she had a choice in the matter.

It wasn't the time to go after Tessa. It really wasn't. She glanced up at me from across the dance floor, her eyes finding mine. I lowered my drink. She lowered the bottle of water she was sipping. Maybe I was looking for it, but I felt the invisible rope between us give a tug. I debated it. If I went to her, I'd be all-in. It was a step I wanted to make, one that was three years overdue.

When I took it, I had to make sure there would be no excuses or things standing in the way. No reason or excuse she could use to hide from me, from us. I stared a moment too long before walking away. Dean was at my side when I walked out the door.

"If it makes you feel any better, Maverick isn't the kid's father."

I knew that already, but I still found myself asking, "What?"

"You said you just wanted to know who the guy was, and when I tried to give you more details, you weren't hearing me." He lit a cigarette and continued, "You ready to hear the rest?"

"Fine, I'll bite. Whose name is on the birth certificate." My throat felt dry all of a sudden. I fought the urge to walk back into that bar and grab another drink. It wouldn't end well. Clearly, I wasn't equipped to handle important information while under the influence of alcohol.

"The father isn't listed and the kid's name is Miles. Miles Frederick Monte."

My throat closed up a bit. *Miles.* Why would she do that? A tiny voice of possibility whispered in my ear, but I shooed it away. When I'd seen her, she hadn't been that far along. When I saw Freddie yesterday, he hadn't given one hint of possibility that I might be the father. Hell, Freddie would've kicked my kneecaps and stabbed me if he had any inkling that I was the father and had been absent all this time. Besides, Samson would've told me.

"What's his birthdate?"

"May fourth."

I felt my jaw tense as I did the math in my head. He was three and change. "Why wouldn't my brother tell me?"

"I thought you told him not to bring her up."

"I did, but he never listened."

"You'd be surprised the things people keep from you for the sake of protection."

"Protection?" I glanced over at him as we walked. "I don't need protection from my son, assuming he is my son, which is highly doubtful."

"I wasn't talking about you." He looked like he might say something more insightful. Instead, he kept it to himself and walked beside me in silence. Why would they think the child would need protection from me? Was I that much like my father? The thought festered inside me the rest of the night.

CHAPTER THIRTEEN

ROWAN

I COULDN'T LET it go. I tossed and turned all night, and it wasn't because of Tessa and Cody's flirting. It was the Miles thing. I'd spent hours trying to reconcile everything, and when the sun rose, I was still right where I started.

At just after six in the morning, someone decided to lean on my doorbell, which was enough to have me out of bed and storming though my house. If this was my brother's idea of a sick joke, I'd kick his ass. Then I'd kick his ass again for not telling me about Miles.

Exhausted, angry, and out of patience, I ripped my front door open and then froze.

"You changed the lock?" Camryn glared, shaking her head. "Seriously?"

"I didn't want you to think I was going to allow you back into my life," I said over my shoulder as I walked into the kitchen, leaving the door open knowing she'd follow. She slammed it behind her, and I stilled in my steps, turning around. "I don't expect you to respect me, but at the very least, respect my house."

"Right, because you can't afford a new door or doorframe."

"That isn't the point, Camryn." I set the coffee to brew. "What do you want?"

"What? A wife can't visit her husband?" She set her over-sized, overpriced bag on the counter and batted her eyelashes.

I crossed my arms and leaned against the counter as I waited for the coffee to brew. Her gaze fell over my naked torso and heated with lust. This wasn't new, and I'd been effectively batting her away for nearly four years, something I'd been proud of because if nothing else the woman could turn a man inside out with her advances.

"What do you want?" I asked again.

"I want to talk about this." She reached into her bag and pulled out a folder, no doubt the divorce papers she had yet to sign. "Why now?"

"Because I have things I need to do, and I can't continue to be stuck in this state of limbo. What do you care? The contract is up soon."

The original contract was up soon, but she'd added in some terms of her own into the prenuptial: if we made it five years or longer, she'd get to keep shares of Hawthorne Industries and because she'd seen the growth the company had, she wanted to cash in on those terms. I'd let it slide before because there was no chance of me meeting another woman I'd want to be serious with.

I'd been too busy with the company and my brother's health to care. The other times I'd asked Camryn for a divorce were the times I'd seen the light or Tessa, sometimes both at once.

I asked for a divorce the week after we got married. I asked again the day after I saw a pregnant Tessa at the conference and again when I saw her a year after that. It seemed she was always at the center of my need for freedom. This time, it was different. This time, I needed Camryn out of my life before the papers for the Hawthorne takeover went through. If she even caught a whiff of what I was doing with the company, she'd never retract her claws, and that was something I couldn't afford. Not with my plans to buy out other companies before the end of the year.

"We still have six months before you're allowed to file. Those were the terms we agreed on," Camryn pointed out, lifting an eyebrow.

"I'm done waiting."

"Why now?" she asked again.

Miles's name came fluttering into my head. Miles, the three-year-old little boy who could very well be my son. I shook the thought away. If he was, why was Cody Maverick pawing her swollen belly? Had he been there when she gave birth? Had he been the first one to look my child in the eyes? And where was Samson during all of this? I tried to excuse my brother. He'd been battling brain cancer, for God's sake, but still. A baby. Possibly *my* baby. I'd never really considered what it would be like to be a father, but the possibility of having that with Tessa didn't seem so bad. I was getting ahead of myself.

"Ro," Camryn snapped.

I turned around and poured some coffee into a mug, paused, sighed, and then reached for a second one. It would be rude of me not to give her some. Hell, maybe it would make her less of a bitch to deal with. I turned, slid a mug to her, and put my elbows on the counter, holding my own warm mug in my hands. She was still obviously checking me out. In times like these, I wondered what her Wall Street boyfriend looked like. Not enough to look him up, but still.

"I need you to sign the papers," I said calmly. "That's all. You act like you want to spend the rest of your life tied down to me or something."

"You act like that isn't an option."

"You—" I stopped myself from reminding her how she'd thrown plates and silverware at me the last time she was here. I needed to stay calm while I dealt with her. "What makes you think it is?"

"I don't know. The fact that I agreed to this ridiculous arrangement is a testament that I don't think us being married is as outlandish as you seem to think."

"Says the woman who spent ninety percent of this marriage with another man."

"Out of necessity." She glanced away. "What am I supposed to do if my own husband won't touch me?"

"I don't think touching or not touching has anything to do with it. You were with him before we signed that contract."

"I left him when I signed it." Her eyes flashed. "I left him for nearly a year, hoping I could be enough for you, but all you did was mope and then fuck other women. Did you think I wouldn't find out about that?"

"I honestly didn't care." I didn't bother correcting her or telling her that her assumptions about me were wrong. There was no point.

"At first, I thought it had to do with Tessa, but it was clear that she was out of your life."

My heart seemed to freeze. "How would you know?"

"You changed your number. Changed your email." She shrugged. "If she were around, you would've probably tried to get these papers sooner." She picked up the folder and waved it around. I said nothing. I didn't want to jeopardize my chance of her signing and getting it over with.

"I don't want to sign the papers," she continued. "I want to try to make this work."

"No. What is it that you really want? More money?"

She glanced away again. "I don't know."

"Well, figure it out, have your attorney jot it down, and send it to mine. We don't need to discuss this."

"I feel like we do."

I set my mug down with a *clunk*. "It's happening. Whether you want to believe it or not, it's happening."

On that note, she picked up her bag and stomped out of the kitchen and my house, slamming the door even harder than she had when she walked in.

CHAPTER FOURTEEN

TESSA

GETTING Miles ready for daycare on Monday was a shit-show. Between my mom saying yes to everything I said no to and him whining that he wanted to stay home with her, I was about ready to lose my mind. As if that weren't enough, I couldn't find my phone anywhere, and I wasn't sure I knew how to survive the subway without it. It had to be in my bag, probably somewhere underneath the baby wipes, NASA spaceships, and Paw Patrol figurines I used to entertain Miles whenever we were out eating and I had to take a call. I picked up Miles's backpack, gave Mom a kiss, and offered him my hand.

"Let's go, Miles."

"I still don't wanna." He crossed his arms, pouting.

Mom smiled and leaned down. "You have to go so that you can come back and teach grandma everything you learned today. When you get back, we'll go to the park and then out for some ice cream with Nana, how 'bout that?"

"Okay." He grinned.

Mom straightened. "I'm going to take a shower and go to Celia's. Mom and I are supposed to go to a wine tasting later."

"And then you're going to the park with Miles?"

"It isn't like I'm driving him anywhere. Besides, some of us can handle our alcohol," she said with a gleam in her eyes. I couldn't help it, I laughed. I'd woken up with the mother of all hangovers yesterday and spent the entire day nursing it and telling everyone around me to shut up.

"Don't remind me."

"You need to get out more, baby," Mom said. "Take advantage of us. We're here to help you. Go have some fun this week."

"I have fun."

"Gymboree doesn't count as fun, Tess." Mom shot me a look. "And Miles needs a father figure in his life." She glanced at Miles, who was walking around the coffee table with a rocket in his hands.

"He has Freddie."

She gave me that sad look I was used to from her. It had been at least a year since the last time she asked who Miles's father was and I was grateful for it because I wasn't sure I had it in me to lie or omit things anymore. I still couldn't believe she hadn't figured it out. Maybe I was fooling myself. Maybe everyone around me knew and they were just playing along for my own sake. I wouldn't be surprised.

"Let's go, Miles," I said. "Thanks, Mom. I'll take you up on the offer."

I held Miles's hand as we walked to the elevator, letting him push the button outside and inside. He was obsessed with buttons and doors and basically everything that had a reaction to his touch. I watched his eyes as they lit up when the elevator started moving. He turned the rocket over upside down to indicate that we were going in that direction. The kid amazed me. "I have a team trying to come up with a concept for a car. Maybe you can help," I told him as the elevator doors opened. "Like cool colors and a theme."

"Like a rocket."

I laughed. Everything was like a rocket to him. "Like a . . ." I stopped walking and looked down at him. He glanced up, sensing this. "Oh my god, Miles. Like a rocket!"

I let go of his hand and rummaged through my messenger bag until I found my small sketchpad that I used to jot down ideas. Miles tugged at my arm as I flipped it open to a fresh page and scribbled: NASA (think: rocket).

"Mommy, there's a man here."

"Just stay by my side and let him get through," I said, only half-listening. If I could get the right blue for the leather and come up with a way that—

Small arms wrapped around my leg. "He keeps looking at me."

My head whipped up, my gaze landing on the glass door and Rowan, who was standing on the other side of it. My pulse spiked. I pushed everything back into my bag, put the strap back on my shoulder and took a hold of Miles's hand again before walking over to the door. I pushed it open. Rowan looked at me for a beat before training his eyes on Miles. I fought the urge to push him behind me and keep him out of sight. This was not how I planned on doing this. Not that I'd composed much of a plan, but if I had, this would not have been it.

"What are you doing here?"

He looked up and held my gaze for entirely too long. Silently, I prayed he wouldn't ask the question I knew he wanted to. I would crack, completely and utterly shatter and tell both him and Miles right then and there.

"I came to pick up the books."

"What books?"

"The books of fabric."

"Oh. Yeah." I blinked. "Um . . . I need to get him to daycare. I can give them to you in like twenty minutes. I can even call Freddie and have him—"

"That's okay. I'll walk with you."

"Walk—" I cleared my throat to clear the squeak from my voice. "You want to walk with us?"

"Sure." His eyes searched mine. "Is there a problem?"

He knew. He knew. He knew. He had to know.

"No. No problem at all."

We started walking.

"What's your name, little man?" Rowan said when he reached the corner. Of course, the walking signal was red. Miles looked at me, then at him, as if to ask whether or not he should tell him. I gave him a nod.

"Miles Frederick Monte."

"Miles, huh?" Rowan's eyes met mine briefly, but in those two seconds, I knew he knew. I just knew it. He looked at Miles. "Nice name. I'm Rowan Andrew Hawthorne."

Had this been an entirely different situation, I would have found his response charming. Miles let go of my hand and offered it for him to shake. Something Freddie and I had been working on with him, and in this moment, I wished like hell I could take it all back. I didn't want them touching. That was a lie. I was just freaking the hell out.

"*Je suis très heureux de faire votre connaissance*," Miles responded, telling Rowan that he was pleased to meet him.

"WHOA." Rowan chuckled, his eyes lighting up. "How old are you?"

"Three," he said.

Rowan gave me another one of those knowing glances, and I turned away.

Fuck my life.

CHAPTER FIFTEEN

ROWAN

THIS TINY LITTLE boy knew French and he was mine. At least I really, really thought he was. I couldn't be sure why I felt that way. Maybe it was his eyes or the way he kept looking at me, suspicious as fuck but also like he knew something. Like we were bonded somehow. I watched Tessa kiss him on both cheeks for the fifth time in a row and hike his little backpack up. He looked at me from over her shoulder and gave a little wave as he walked away.

"He's smart," I said when she was next to me again.

"They want to promote him a grade, but I'm scared it'll hurt him in the long run."

"How so?" We started walking in the opposite direction, back to her apartment for those books I could've cared less about.

"You know how older kids are. I don't want him to get picked on because he'd be younger, smaller, smarter."

"What does his father say?" I eyed her closely.

She was shaking. Her hands, her body, even her smile. She was definitely keeping something from me. The awful thought that maybe Sam was his father crossed my mind, but if that were the case, he wouldn't have kept it from me. As much as he knew it would hurt me, he would have told me. I didn't think my brother would do that to me, not after everything.

I crossed my arms. I'd just ask her straight out. I mean, I'd ask if the kid was mine, she'd say no, I'd deal with it. It wasn't as if I'd ever considered having children, but the thought had been there and gone. Camryn and I sure as hell never spoke about it. I couldn't even imagine having a child with her, but a child with Tessa? The idea didn't really seem all that terrible. I summoned the question and allowed myself to ask it, keeping my eyes on hers.

"Is he mine?"

"What?" She stumbled back slightly but then caught herself and straightened.

"Is he mine?"

"Why would you ask that?" Her voice was hoarse.

Holy shit.

He was mine. I felt my own throat closing up. If he wasn't, she would have laughed, said no quickly, and then told me to go fuck myself. Instead, she looked to be at a loss for words. I swallowed thickly and asked again. All this time I'd held out hope that maybe someday I could go after this woman and make things between us work, despite thinking she had a child with someone else, despite thinking she'd moved on quickly after me, and the entire time she'd been keeping this secret from me? Keeping him from me? I needed to hear her say it.

"Is he?"

She brought her hands up and pressed her face into them, nodding. I reached out and grabbed her arm, pulling her off to the side, away from the crowd walking the street. She kept her face in her hands. I stared at the top of her head, wondering why I wasn't full of rage or overflowing with anger because she'd kept him from me.

What I felt was an intense pressure in my breastbone, something akin to sadness, longing. Things I couldn't quite place. After years of feeling like I was on top of the world, I suddenly felt small and lost.

Funny how another person's actions could make you feel that way. A son. *My son.* I thought about her pregnant, about Cody Maverick's hands all over her stomach when it should have been mine. My chest squeezed tighter with each passing second.

"Why would you keep this from me?"

"You'd just gotten married," she whispered. "What were you going to do? Give it all up because I was pregnant?"

"Yes."

She shot me a disbelieving look. I didn't blame her. Thinking back, I probably wouldn't have given any of it up. Not because I didn't want to. Deep down, I was just looking for an excuse, something to make me throw in the towel and walk away, chase after her.

"You would have been miserable," she said. "And you would have blamed your son for it."

She might as well have slapped me; that was how much her words stung. She thought I'd blame a child for my failures? For not being able to keep my end of the bargain and doing what I'd been molded to do? Maybe she was right. Maybe I was that person, like my father, unable to take responsibility for my own actions without blaming those around me. We continued to stare at each other. She looked cagey, as if she would take out the claws I knew she hid well and strike at any given moment. Despite the pain I felt, I wasn't about to stand down.

"Am I that horrible?" I whispered. "That you wouldn't think I'd at least want to know that I fathered a child?"

"This isn't about you." She wiped the tears that continuously streamed down her face. "I swear it isn't."

"Then who is it about?" I shouted. "You've kept this secret for three fucking years. Does my brother know?"

"He just found out," she whispered. "He didn't know."

"Bullshit!"

"I swear he didn't know. No one knows."

My eyes narrowed. *Bullshit.* The kid looked just like me. I didn't believe for one second my brother didn't know. He'd obviously been in the child's life all this time. I wondered if he'd been there for his first cry and his first laugh. His first word. I wondered how many firsts he'd accomplished. The kid knew French, so it was clear he'd accomplished a lot more than I could conjure in two seconds. It wasn't as if I knew anything about toddlers, but that kid was clearly brilliant.

I had a son. A smart, adorable, son named Miles. And the woman I had dreamed of every night since the day I let her go had kept him from me. I pinched the bridge of my nose.

"I can't believe this."

"Sam just found out, and I asked him not to tell you," she whispered.

"Why?"

"Because I needed time to figure out how I would do it," she said, her voice shaking with each word she spoke. She shut her eyes as if looking at me while saying this was becoming unbearable for her.

"Why didn't you tell me, Tessa?"

"You made it pretty clear you wanted nothing to do with me the day we saw each other in the courthouse. I gave you my heart on a platter and you tossed it out the window."

"That doesn't mean—"

"You changed your phone number!" She continued, her voice breaking with each word. "I called and you'd changed it."

I had. I'd changed it because I didn't want the temptation of her voice to lure me away from my goals and in turn mess up hers. Still. She had a fucking son. My son. And kept him from me.

"I saw you," I argued. "I saw you twice. You had the chance to tell me in person."

"When? Before or after you stopped holding your wife's hand and parading her around the building like she was made of glass? Should I have told you in front of her? Made a family meeting out of it?"

"So instead of trying to find the right time you shut me out of his life?"

"What difference would it have made? You married the devil your mother hates me—" She exhaled shakily. "Do you really think I'd trust either of those women in a room with Miles unless I was there?"

"What about me?" I asked loudly. "You could have trusted me."

"How?" she whispered. I swallowed the blow the word brought with it.

"We could have—" I breathed out, running a hand through my hair. "Jesus, Tessa."

"I know it's a lot to take in, but this is my son, and I need to do what's best for him."

"Meaning leaving me out of his life."

"Meaning leaving anyone who isn't good for him out of his

life. It isn't about you! It's about people around you, like your wife, who posts pictures of herself on Instagram that clearly show lines of coke in the background. That isn't the kind of environment I want my son around."

My jaw clenched. "She is not my wife."

"You said you're in the process of getting a divorce, which means she still is."

"She won't be my wife much longer and you have known all along that it has been a marriage of convenience."

"It doesn't matter what it was or what it wasn't. She lives with you. She shares a bed with you. A life with you. I don't want her anywhere near my son."

I didn't bother to tell her that she was wrong, that we didn't live together and hadn't shared a bed for the majority of our marriage. "So, what am I supposed to do? Forget this conversation happened and move on?"

"Until the divorce is final, yes."

"You can't be serious." I stared at her. Her expression was set and unwavering. She was being dead serious. "That can take months."

She shrugged, looking away as if to say it wasn't her problem. Beneath the sadness and self-loathing, rage finally simmered.

"I can file for custody," I said. "He's my son."

"Is he?" Her eyes flared. "You'd have to prove that he is, which would mean convincing a court to grant you a paternity test. Is that what you want to do to your son?"

"If it's what it takes."

"What it takes for *what*, Rowan?" she raised her voice. "You're on top of the world. You have it all. What could you possibly want from us?"

A family.

It was the first thought that came to mind. I wasn't even sure what a family entailed, but I wanted one—a real one, and I wanted it with her. I couldn't say that because it wasn't the time and definitely not the place. Tessa was on the defense as it was.

"I want my son."

Her bottom lip trembled. She bit it and glanced away. "I need time."

"Time? You've had nothing but time. I have time to make up for."

"I can't just spring this on him." Her bewildered gaze met mine. "You can't just waltz up here and claim him as yours. Why do you think I didn't show up at your doorstep?"

"Because the thought of seeing another woman holding his hand blinded you from reality."

Her hand came up in a quick thunderous move I didn't see coming until the sting of the slap made my face turn. I brought my hand up and glared at her, taking a deep breath to calm myself.

"Don't you dare accuse me of being jealous. You don't have a clue what I've been through and given up in order to keep Miles safe."

"I saw you when you were pregnant. I saw Cody Maverick rubbing your stomach like Miles was his." My throat closed again. My face stung beneath the palm of my hand, and I continued to glare at her. "Do you know how it feels to know that all of these men have been in my son's life? All this time?"

"I'm sorry," she whispered, blinking away tears.

"Sorry?" I squeezed my eyes shut. "I hurt you when I sent you away. I hurt myself that day, too, trust me. But this, Tess?" I looked at her again. "This is the worst kind of pain I've ever felt."

I closed my eyes again and focused on my breathing.

"I need to calm down and I can't do that with you standing in front of me." I needed to get away from her, from this street, from wandering eyes . . . and everything. I said as much and walked away.

CHAPTER SIXTEEN

TESSA

I DIDN'T GO to work. I skipped the Monday meeting with Ryan Ford and stayed home, balled up in bed crying hysterically. Mom and Joan were gone for the day, so when my front door opened and Celia called out for me, I pulled the covers over my head and prayed she was just stealing kitchen supplies like she often did when she was too lazy to take a trip to the grocery store. My bedroom door squeaked.

"Tess?" she said. "Chloe's here to bring you soup. Why didn't you tell me you were sick?"

I feigned sleep. She wouldn't know the difference. The sheets were pulled away, and I covered my face, but not quickly enough.

She gasped, lowering my hands. "What happened?"

I opened my eyes, saw the concern in her eyes, and started to cry again. "I really messed up. I think. I don't know."

"What? How? What happened?"

"R-R-Ro knows."

"About Miles?" Her eyes widened. She glanced up again.

"What do you mean he knows about Miles? What does that mean?" Freddie's voice boomed from the doorway. As if I could possibly hide from this, I squeezed my eyes closed and pulled myself into a tight ball.

"Rowan is Miles's dad," Celia answered when I didn't.

"I thought you said she had a one-night stand with some guy." He walked in, glaring at Celia and then pulled my arm away from my face. "What the fuck, Tessa?"

"Freddie, just—"

"Don't *just* me, Celia. Move."

"I'm just going to leave the soup on the counter," Chloe called out.

"Thanks, Chlo," I managed as I sat up and wiped my face. Freddie drew the blinds, letting the sun in. Out of all the days the sun decided to grace us with its presence, it had to pick today.

"Your face is swollen," Celia said. "I'm going to get some ice packs."

Freddie crossed his arms, looming over me. If he weren't my protective older brother, I would've cowered. His dark hair was perfectly brushed back and his caramel eyes were more pronounced than usual in the sunlight. Or maybe it was because I was trying to keep my eyes on his and not his hardened jaw.

"He didn't know," I said meekly.

"I got that. Why didn't you tell me, though? Why did you lie to *me?*" He stepped forward and sat beside me on the bed. "I'm your brother. How can you just not tell me?"

"I kept it from his father," I said, my voice barely a whisper, hoping that would be enough to excuse me from not telling him.

"I'm your brother." He exhaled and shook his head. "But while we're at it, why didn't you tell him?"

"It just—" Tears swam in my eyes again, the weight of the burden pushed against my throat. "It seems so stupid now."

"It isn't stupid," Celia said, walking back into the room. She crouched beside the bed next to me and held my gaze as she brought an ice pack to my cheeks. "Miles is your priority. I'm tired of people judging women who genuinely don't need men in their lives."

"Don't start," Freddie warned.

"He wants to file for custody," I interrupted. Her eyes widened. She pressed the pack a little harder.

"And as the only man in this room, I feel inclined to add that if I were Rowan, I'd be furious and file for joint custody too."

"He doesn't even know him." My gaze flashed to Freddie's and I let him see every bit of anger and ferocity inside me. "This hasn't ever been about keeping Miles away from Rowan. It has always been about keeping Miles away from Camryn. I don't trust her not to do something bad to him. I won't risk my son and there is nothing you or anyone else could possibly say to get me to change my mind."

Truthfully, if I took everyone else out of the equation, there was nothing I wanted more than for Rowan to be in Miles's life. I thought about how bad his asthma got when he was sick and how he needed to be monitored for his nebulizer. Rowan would be such a responsible father if he ever came around to the idea of actually being a father. Maybe he was pissed off at me for keeping the secret but had no intention of doing anything about it. Who the hell knew? He did, that was who. I'd have to confront him about all of this, but not yet.

"I understand that," Freddie said. "And I'm sure Ro would have, too, if you told him."

"I tried."

"Try again." After a long, quiet moment, his soulful eyes searching mine, he said, "You loved him once. What happened?"

"Life happened," Celia said, but my eyes stayed on my brother's. It was a fair question and "life happened" wasn't a fair answer. I owed him as much honesty as I could.

"He chose work and Camryn over me," I said. "And between work and Miles and Sam's health and everything else in between, I just . . ." I shrugged, trying to keep my throat from closing up.

Truth was, it felt like thirty years not four. And yet, I'd never stopped loving him. Not for a second. Freddie's large hand came down on top of mine. Celia's covered my other hand. I wondered if Rowan had called Sam for comfort and support or if he'd done his usual and handled this in private. I wondered if he would confide in Camryn. The thought didn't bother me the way it normally would have, not when I had so much moral support from my brother and sister and I knew the way Rowan was. How long would it take him to digest these feelings?

"Do you think I should go to him and apologize, offer to let them get to know each other?"

"Give him time," Freddie said. Celia nodded in agreement.

"Why don't you go to the cottage for a few days and regroup?"

"I have huge projects right now," I said, though the cottage sounded amazing.

"So, work from there." Freddie shrugged. "Mom and Joan will be here, I'm here for the next few weeks. Celia will be here until her poetry book launches in a few months. We got Miles covered."

"Disparity is an artist's best friend," Celia added. Freddie chuckled, nodding in agreement.

It sounded like a good plan. I mulled it over. I'd have to go into the office and sort things out before I did that, but I stood and called my grandmother, who sounded worried but didn't ask any questions. She just told me to take the keys and go. That was what family did—offer things that would make your life easier without asking for anything in return. I thought about Miles and the way we all worked so hard to instill that in him. I didn't want to think negative thoughts about letting Rowan into his life, but negative thoughts were all I could conjure. It was unfair, I knew this, but I couldn't seem to turn it off.

CELIA HAD INSISTED on coming with me to the office, claiming she would take the opportunity to visit her publishing house and sign some books and promo material while she was there. I think we both knew it was a lame excuse, but I didn't argue with her.

"This is nice," she said when we exited the elevator on my floor. She'd only seen pictures of my office, but I had yet to bring Miles or let anyone else come visit for that matter. Too many things were happening too fast in every aspect of my life. Groaning, I slowed down as I passed Ryan Ford's office. Of course, today of all days, he was sitting behind his desk.

"I have to go in here," I whispered to Celia.

She read the nameplate on the door, nodded, and said, "Got it. I'll be in your office. It's the one down the hall, right?"

"Right-hand corner."

She gave me a thumbs-up and kept walking. I knocked on the door and waited for him to invite me in. When I heard his voice boom, I pushed the door open and peeked my head in. He looked up from his desk, looking every bit as gorgeous and composed as I'd expected him to look.

"You look like hell," he said by way of greeting. I felt my brows rise.

"That is not something you're supposed to say to someone you just met." I stepped into his office and closed the door behind me. He stood, offering me his hand to shake. I gripped a little extra for good measure.

"Well, you do look like hell, and you missed our team meeting." He sat, and I took the seat across from him. "What's going on?"

"Something came up," I said. "A major something, obviously."

"Obviously." He sounded bored. "Major enough to have you come in late, looking like hell, with a sidekick in tow."

I glanced over my shoulder. The hall was empty, but duh, glass windows. He'd seen Celia. I faced him again. "That's my sister, and yes, a sidekick was necessary."

"So, you're here to tell me you're taking time off in the middle of the biggest projects we may ever work on."

"Says the man who didn't show up for the first week of work because he was on vacation." I crossed my arms because I wasn't about to take shit from him about time off. He leaned back in his seat, watching me closely. I wouldn't wither, especially not after the day I'd had.

"How long will you be gone?"

"The rest of the week and I'll be working from home." I shot him a look as I said that last part. He seemed to be having a difficult time not smiling.

"These projects can't pause," he said.

"They won't. I'm going to meet with my team right now and cover all the bases before I go."

"Perfect," he said. I stood. He followed suit, clearly trained in being a gentleman. He shook my hand again. "It was nice to finally meet you. I've heard a lot of great things from Yamina and Rowan Hawthorne, so I'm looking forward to working with you."

I blinked. "I'm surprised Rowan would have anything good to say about me at all."

Ryan smiled like he knew a little too much for my comfort. "All good things."

Somehow, I doubted that, but I managed to walk out of the office without asking. I passed Chloe in the hallway and told her to get the rest of the team for a quick meeting. When I walked into my office, Celia was sitting in my chair with her hands behind her head and her booted feet crossed on my desk.

"What are you doing?"

"This office is everything and I have always wanted to do this," she said, lowering her feet and straightening in the chair. "It gives me *Wolf of Wall Street* vibes."

I laughed. "I don't want those vibes in here. We're already stressed."

"Who's Ryan Ford?"

"The guy I was just talking to. He's the acquisitions director and also Rowan's friend."

Her brows rose. "Interesting. Is he cute?"

"Very. He also looks like the kind of man who doesn't look like he'd have a single tattoo and probably has a harem waiting at his beck and call. Basically, not your type."

"Sounds like way too much trouble." Her lips pursed. "Anyway, I'm on a dating website. I'll find love one way or another."

I shook my head as I set my messenger bag onto the small conference table and took my sketchbook out. "I don't understand why anyone would work so hard to find love when love was the ultimate letdown."

"You only say that because you've been in love with the same person your entire life."

"And look at what it's done for me."

"Love gave you Miles."

Her words gripped my chest. She was right. Miles was the most beautiful, incredible person in the universe.

The door opened and Chloe, Tommy, and Seth walked in, effectively ending my and Celia's conversation. My sister finally got out of my chair, did a quick introduction, and gave me a kiss goodbye.

"I'll pack your bag," she said. "Freddie's filling up the tank."

I wrapped my arms around her and held her tight, fighting back a new wave of tears. You'd think I would've run out of them, but they were still there. "Thank you."

When she left, closing the door behind her, I watched her through the glass and waited until I was fully calm before facing my team and getting straight to work.

CHAPTER SEVENTEEN

ROWAN

I HADN'T SEEN my father in nearly a year, so I could only imagine how surprised he was when I showed up on his doorstep. If I had to guess, it would probably be about as shocked as I was to be standing there.

"Is everything okay?"

"No," I said. "I'm here to tell you how not okay things are and why you're the reason for it."

His brows rose. "That may take a while. You want to come inside?"

I walked past him for two reasons: it was cold and I didn't

drive all the way out here just to leave. My eyes scanned everything as I followed him to the kitchen. He'd moved into this house with Mariah and the half-brother I had but hadn't met. My brother had. Of course, he'd met him. He'd also forgiven my father for being an awful, no-good man and welcomed his new wife and son with open arms. Sam was a better man than I was and his cancer diagnosis had made him re-evaluate everything in his life. He'd said that to me once and while I understood it, I couldn't imagine myself doing the same if I was in his position.

The kitchen was homey, with kitchen towels that said things like "Chop it like it's hot" and "Don't go bacon my heart." Shit, my dad never would have allowed those in my mother's kitchen. He sat on a stool. I stood. I wasn't about to make myself comfortable.

Hell, I wanted him to be as uncomfortable as I felt, but that didn't look as if it were going to happen.

"I just found out that I have a son," I said, cutting through the bullshit. He leaned forward and rubbed his jaw. "And of all the emotions that are supposed to come with that knowledge, the one I keep going back to is uncertainty. My entire life I have told myself I wouldn't become you and it took me this long to realize that maybe I already have. All I do is work and think about the company. I haven't taken a vacation or a sick day in five years, and even though I was completely blindsided by the knowledge of a son, I haven't once in the last twenty-four hours made an effort to go see him."

"How old is he?" Dad asked. He seemed to be having trouble getting the words out.

"A little over three."

He glanced away momentarily, when his blue eyes met mine again, they looked wary. "I don't know what you want me to tell you, Rowan. I can apologize, like I did with Sam, but I have a feeling that I can sit here and apologize until I'm blue in the face, and you'd still hate me."

"You never once hugged us," I said. "You never once told us you loved us or that you were proud of us."

"And for that, I'm sorry. I'm not sure if you've been paying attention, but I didn't grow up with an incredible father either."

I swallowed. "That's my fear. You didn't break the cycle. How can I be sure I will?"

"You can't be sure." He shrugged. "What does your mother say?"

"I haven't told her."

"Does Sam know?"

"He knew before I did."

Realization flickered in his eyes. "Tessa's boy."

Tessa's boy. Why did my heart skip a beat when he said that? I nodded once but kept quiet because I knew when Dad wasn't done talking and for once, I wanted to hear what he had to say.

"I haven't met him," he said. "Sam talks about him often and I keep in touch with the Montes. They're crazy about their grandson." He smiled as he said that but then sobered. "I'm assuming Camryn doesn't know."

I tensed. This was it. I'd given him the perfect opportunity to get back at me for all the awful things I'd said to him. For every time I'd thrown his extramarital affair and illegitimate son in his face. I waited, the anxiety bunching between my shoulder blades.

"Why don't you take a seat?" he asked instead. I swallowed past the lump that seemed to have become a permanent fixture in my throat and dropped onto the seat across from him.

"My life is different," he said with a chuckle, waving a hand. "I know you can see the difference, but I don't just mean this. I mean everything has changed. I've changed and I'm sorry that you and your brother got the short end of the stick and grew up while I still had a lot of growing up to do myself. You have to understand that I did the best that I could. It's all we can do."

"I don't know the first thing about being a father." I clenched my jaw to get a hold of my emotions.

Dad smiled. "Neither do I and here I am, doing it for a third time."

I tore my gaze from his. My eyes landed on a picture of him, Mariah, and a little boy all smiling at the camera. It was his smile that nearly broke my heart in two. It looked genuine. Dad looked older than he did in family pictures when I was a kid and ten times happier. He was actually smiling. Really smiling, eyes crinkling with amusement. The three of them looked so . . . happy.

"He's a good kid. Reminds me a lot of you," he said and my throat closed up because it was the first nice thing about me that he'd ever said. "He tries so hard to please me and you know what? He does, just like you did when you were his age."

He gestured toward the pictures hanging on his wall, and I nod, spotting the few he had of Sam and me.

"I speak to him about you. Sam comes around often enough, but Harrison is always asking about you. It's as if he relates to you even though he's only ever seen photographs of you." I could hear the smile in his voice, but I didn't acknowledge it because I wasn't sure that I could without bleeding emotions all over the damn place.

I didn't bleed.

But I did crack.

"Maybe I can meet him sometime." The words left my mouth before I had a chance to stop them.

"I'd like that." He paused momentarily. "How's the company? Did your grandparents sign the contract?"

"It's been with their lawyer for weeks, but they'll sign it. I'm offering more than the company's worth." I didn't have to since I owned a higher percentage than they did at the moment. After I took over as CEO, I made it so that they couldn't really see the entirety of our profit, so they didn't know that I was paying them less than they were worth. It was sneaky, yes, but that was the way they liked to play, and I wasn't going to let anything get in the way of this.

"You'll get it," he said. "What's going on with the contract? Is Camryn ready to get out?"

I scoffed. "She's refusing to sign the papers."

"Does she think you have a chance at a real family?"

"She already moved out. Not entirely by choice, but it isn't like we ever acted like a real couple," I said. Dad raised his eyebrows in response. "She just wants control."

"Maybe she knows something's up."

"She wouldn't." I shook my head. The last thing I needed was for her to find out about Miles and make this more difficult than it already was.

"You need to be careful. I'm assuming if Tessa didn't tell you about him it was for a reason."

"She saw a picture of Camryn at a party or somewhere and there was cocaine in the picture," I said by way of explanation. I'd never condoned drug usage. I'd always been far too involved in my health and fitness to want to put a substance like that into my body, but to someone like Camryn cocaine was like having a social cigarette. I said this to my father, but he looked doubtful.

"I wouldn't want my son around that either," he said finally.

"Like I said, Camryn moved out months ago, and even before then she'd been carrying on an affair with some guy in the city. She was barely home." I closed my eyes. It didn't matter what I said or how I justified any of it, I'd lost three years with my son and couldn't blame anyone but myself for it. "I need to find a way to fix all of this. I guess I can figure out the how to be a father thing later."

Dad leaned back in his seat. "Do you remember how you felt about me when you were little?"

My first thought was to say I hated him, but that wasn't quite right. I truly hadn't started holding a grudge against him until I found out about the affair and the kid he had. Before then, I'd looked up to him, despite it all.

"I wanted to be just like you."

"Kids don't see parents as good or bad. You can be the worst person in the world and your children won't realize it until they're faced with the same situation and it suddenly clicks that maybe their father wasn't right to tell his child that he didn't bleed," he said, a sense of sorrow in his eyes.

"Maybe I wasn't right to push you the way I did or take my own unhappiness out on you. Maybe I should've let you sleep in and go to the baseball field with your brother. I made so many mistakes, Rowan. Sometimes I sit and look at the pictures of you and your brother and wish I could go back and fix it all. I'd try to be more loving and show you how important you are. I'd treat you the way you deserve to be treated. I'd hug you and thank you for saving me, because you did, you saved me every damn Saturday because having you in my passenger seat ensured that I wouldn't drive off a cliff. You can judge me all you want. You have every right to. But you can't know the pain that lived inside me, a pain you had nothing to do with even if I made you feel that way sometimes. I can't go back and right my wrongs, son, but I can apologize today and try to be a better father going forward."

He stood and came around the table. I sat with a clenched stomach, unsure of what was happening, and then he wrapped his arms around me and gave me a hug. I was bigger than my father, taller, more muscular, but in that moment, I felt small. In that moment, I felt like a needy six-year-old.

"I'm sorry," he said in a hoarse voice against my hair. "I'll try to be a better man."

Something inside me shattered. Tears rolled down my face without preamble. I heard him exhale onto me, but his arms never let up, and I realized that this was what I'd been waiting for my entire life, and the only thing I managed to do was hope that I could provide the same for someone else.

CHAPTER EIGHTEEN

TESSA

MY GRANDMOTHER'S three-bedroom cottage sat up on a hill
and had a fully renovated basement that held a wine cellar and
theatre room. The latter was her way of trying to bribe Freddie to
visit more often. It never worked. Not because he didn't want to
visit but because he was too busy with The Company. When he
wasn't at work, he was painting. I wish he'd quit his day job and
just paint forever, but like he had said, you shouldn't put all your
eggs in one basket.

Earlier, as I brainstormed with Seth and Tommy over the
phone, I'd gone downstairs to the cellar and picked out a bottle of

red. It was one the Chateau made as an exclusive a few years back. All they did was change the label, but it had been enough to get the attention of a Prime Minister, which had the sales skyrocketing. That didn't really matter to me since I knew next to nothing about wine, but the bottle was a cabernet so I'd taken it.

I stood from the couch, where I'd been sitting and flipping through fabrics since I'd ended the call, headed to the kitchen to open said bottle and order a pizza. Then I looked outside, it was too cool out, definitely not the kind of weather I'd take the canoe out in, but I wished I could. Grandma Joan had renovated the cottage a couple of years ago, tearing down the wall that faced the water and replacing it with glass. The view was truly spectacular and I could picture Miles's beloved telescope sitting right there by that glass. Celia told me Rowan and Sam had passed by to pick up the other books and had spent a few minutes with Miles. A part of me hated that I hadn't been there for it, to take pictures, even if only just to store in my memory bank. The other part of me was glad I wasn't there because I wasn't sure I'd be able to hold it together. The need to apologize to Rowan ran deep and I didn't have time for distractions, especially when I still hadn't settled on any of the fabrics. I picked up my wine and walked back over to the book of fabrics and the hundreds of sketches scattered around it. At least I got that part right. The couches for the hotel design were simple, but the colors I had in mind were bold and bright—royal blues and bright yellows. A Moroccan theme. I'd have to discuss it with Seth and Tommy at nine o'clock during our Skype. I set those aside and went back to the spring collection, which I'd finished sketching. I emailed Seth and Tommy everything earlier, and even though I knew the sketches were great, I was nervous about their feedback. This was my new team. I'd rocked it in Prim Paris, but what if they hated everything I did?

The doorbell rang. I set the sketches down and picked up my

wallet, my grumbling stomach reminding me just how hungry I was as I walked over to the door. I pulled it open and did a double take when I saw Rowan standing on the other side, wearing jeans, a long-sleeve white shirt, and a New York Rangers cap.

"What are you doing here?"

"I'm missing a fabric book."

"You drove three hours for a fabric book?"

"I went to pick up the others and your grandmother told me you were holed up here. I wanted to see if you were okay."

"Why?" I eyed him suspiciously. If he was here to talk about splitting custody, I'd turn him away. It wasn't that I wasn't open to the conversation, because I knew that conversation was inevitable and necessary. I'd come here to get my head straight and I wasn't there yet. His eyes narrowed as if he was mulling over what to say next.

"I came to apologize."

"Really?"

Out of all the things he could have said, that was the one that surprised me the most. I'd kept his son a secret from him and he was apologizing to me?

"For what?"

"Can we discuss this inside? I'm freezing."

I bit my tongue. How many times had we played this song and dance? Something about it felt different this time. Years ago, I would have moved out of the way and melted under those blue eyes, but I had become harder. I'd learned life lessons and grown up, so despite my galloping heart and the pulse that was skittering, I didn't feel the need to make room for him as easily as I once would have. Eventually, after staring at each other for what felt like a solid two minutes, I moved. He walked inside slowly, looking around, taking it all in.

"This is nice."

"It is." I watched his broad back as he stood there and finally closed the door. My stomach growled again.

He turned around. "You hungry?"

"Very."

"Want me to go get food? I thought about bringing something, but I didn't want to get ahead of myself."

"I ordered pizza. It should be here any minute."

He nodded once, sliding his hands into his pockets and rocking back on his heels. "Are you still working?"

"If I wasn't, I would've gone home already."

He moved to where the book was open to the blue swatches and touched the sketches. I didn't want his fingers on them. It was too personal, too much hurt came from the simple gesture, and I rushed over and stood in front of the coffee table, blocking his view. Unfortunately, it put me almost chest to chest with him. The scent of his cologne, his shampoo, body wash, *him*, infiltrated my senses. Our gazes collided and in that one tiny second, I felt it all rushing back to me and wished so badly I could forget about the past and jump on him. It was the wine, anxiety, and lack of action for sure. I knew he saw this, too, with the way his nostrils flared as he looked at me.

"Tessa."

I glanced away, ignoring the way the rasp in his voice made everything inside me vibrate. "Please don't look at my sketches."

"You always let me look at your sketches."

I met his gaze again. "How can you say that with a straight face as if you did nothing wrong?" The doorbell rang. I went to move, but Rowan grabbed my arm, his eyes narrowing slightly.

"What's that supposed to mean?"

"You know what it's supposed to mean." I yanked my arm free, grabbed the cash on the table, and went to get my dinner.

When Rowan saw just how much I had ordered, his eyes narrowed. "Are you expecting someone?"

"No." I walked over to the kitchen. "Why?"

"How much food did you get?"

"One pizza, one dessert pizza, and garlic rolls. Why?"

He dragged his eyes over my body slowly and back up. "Where do you store all of this food?"

"None of your business. Besides, I was starving when I ordered and you know I eat with my eyes."

He helped me set the table. For two, of course, because Rowan was the kind of guy who invited himself into your life, your heart, and your table. I rolled my eyes but said nothing. I was torn between wishing I still wanted to apologize and wanted to ring his neck, and the longer I could smell him, see him, hear him, the more the latter seemed like the option I would take. He served me the first slice and then grabbed one for himself before refilling my wine glass.

"You're glaring at me." I was.

"I'm picturing your head exploding."

He barked out a surprised laugh, a real one that lit up his eyes and showcased that perfect grin of his. "Tell me how you really feel."

"You couldn't handle it."

He laughed again.

"It isn't funny."

"It kind of is. The entirety of this situation—from Miles to you feeling like I somehow wronged you by looking at a sketch—is borderline hysterical."

I exhaled a breath. Fine. He wanted to ask about how I really felt, I would tell him. But first . . .

"Why'd you email me the pictures?"

"What pictures?" He bit into a slice of pizza.

"The wedding pictures."

"What are you—" He frowned, shaking his head. "What wedding pictures? Why would I email you wedding pictures?"

"I got an email from you shortly after I got to Paris," I said. "Attached to it were pictures of you and Camryn. She was wearing a wedding dress. I can't even tell you what you were wearing."

"I sent those to you?"

"Yes."

I watched as he took another bite of pizza and then chewed slowly, studying my face as I did his, looking for any kind of reaction.

"Tessa, I didn't email you those pictures."

I grabbed my phone and scrolled through it, knowing that despite the fact that Celia begged me to delete the email and move on, I'd find it quickly because I never had. Whenever I had a moment of weakness and wanted to try to get in touch with him, I opened the email and reminded myself why I couldn't. Once I had the image pulled up, I tossed my phone to him. He dropped his pizza and caught it before it hit his chest.

"You wanna know why I didn't tell you I was pregnant? Why I didn't tell you I'd had your baby the time I saw you at that conference? That's why."

He looked at the pictures for a second before setting the phone aside and looking at me again. I was sure that was sorrow I saw in his eyes, but I was past the point of caring, my blood was past the point of boiling.

"God, Rowan." My voice fell to a whisper. "She was wearing a dress identical to the sketch I'd ripped out of my sketchbook, which looked fucking ridiculous on her, by the way, but that isn't the point. The point is that you let her have that dress made, took pictures with her in it, and then sent them to me. For what? To rub it all in my face? I couldn't have you and you wanted me to make sure I really understood it? To make sure I'd move on and not look back?" My voice rose with each word and I really didn't give a damn. "It wasn't enough that I told you I loved you and you acted like it was the worst thing in the world? Did you change your number and email for her benefit too? Because when I was pregnant and alone and fucking scared and tried to reach out to you, you were gone!"

"You could've told Sam," he said, his voice barely a whisper. Hot, angry tears pricked my eyes, I blinked, and they fell down my face.

"Sam? When? Before or after chemo? Before or after he was fighting for his goddamn life? Jesus, Rowan." I shook my head, disappointed. He'd never change. He'd come to apologize, but he didn't mean it. He just wanted to do the socially acceptable thing. "Besides, if Sam had reached out to you and told you and you'd said no? That would have killed me. I couldn't deal with more heartache. First you, then my pregnancy, then Sam's health. It was too much."

Rowan pushed his chair back and stood, walked around the table and crouched beside me. I tried to avert my eyes to the floor, to the black sneakers he wore, but he brought his hand up and brushed my hair behind my ear and I found myself glancing up to meet his gaze.

"I would never send you those pictures," he said.

"Which means she did. And you expect me to be okay with that kind of person around my son?"

"I don't." He lowered his hand and placed it over mine on my lap. "I don't want her around him either. You have to trust me on that. I'm sorry about everything I said the other day. I was taken by surprise and I just didn't know how to handle it all. I changed my phone number and email for my sake, because the thought of reaching out to you haunted me every morning and every night."

He reached up and cupped my face, wiping the tear that trickled down my cheek with his thumb. "You've always had me, Sprite," he whispered. "Even from across the pond, despite all the lies and deception, you'll always have me."

"How can you possibly say that?"

"Because it's the truth." He smiled sadly, tilting his head. "And I didn't recognize the dress from your sketch. I'm sorry that you had to deal with any of that, but I would never do that. How could you think I would?"

"I thought maybe you wanted me to see them before they were published in a newspaper or magazine. I don't know."

"Those pictures were taken for my grandparents to make things look official. They were never meant to be published anywhere." He threaded his fingers through mine. "And I sure as fuck wouldn't have let her wear a dress I thought you designed."

"You really had no clue?" I searched his eyes. How could he not know?

"I wasn't in the best state of mind those days. I'd just let you go. How could I be?"

"I don't want her near my son," I repeated.

"I don't either, but I want to know him. I don't have a fucking clue what I'm doing, but I want to try."

"It isn't a game," I said. "I'm only here right now because my mom, grandmother, Celia, and Freddie are with Miles, and they're the only people I trust with anything in the world. Parenthood is twenty-four seven. Always on call even when you don't want to show up to work. There are no sick days or one more minute in bed to get some rest."

"Please let me be in your lives," he said. "I'll follow your lead and respect your boundaries."

"Okay."

He smiled. I smiled despite the uncertainty.

The alarm on my phone rang, indicating that it was time for my Skype call. I said as much to Rowan, who stood, taking my hand and pulling me with him. When I was on my feet, he lifted my knuckles to his lips and brushed a soft kiss against each peak.

The feel of his soft bottom lip against my knuckles made my nerve endings go haywire. My phone vibrated.

"I really have to work." I managed to say the words above the swooshing in my ears.

"Can I watch?"

"You need to promise you'll behave."

He nipped the tips of my fingers one by one, keeping his gaze locked on mine. "I always behave."

CHAPTER NINETEEN

ROWAN

IF I'D KNOWN Camryn did that with the sketch I kept inside my wallet I would have . . . I didn't know what I would have done. I'd already married her when those pictures were taken. I couldn't have divorced her because of an email. Even if I had known about Miles back then, I couldn't say with certainty I would have divorced her.

I had needed time. I had needed the moment I saw Tessa, pregnant with what I thought was another man's baby, to set in motion what became years of sorrow and loneliness. Years in which I kicked myself continuously for not at least verbally acknowledging the feelings I had for her. I needed that pain to give me the perspective to really understand that there hadn't been another way. Sitting here, I knew that the man I was four years ago had done the right thing, because without my doing that, I wouldn't know what I know today. I wouldn't have grown or changed or altered my direction.

I cleared the table while she sat in the living room Skyping with the guys she worked with. I did the dishes and drank my wine in the kitchen. When I went by Tessa's apartment and Joan told me she was here, she gave me permission to take the guest room and make myself at home. Freddie mentioned a movie theatre room in the basement. I didn't want to move too far away from Tessa, still feeling like we still had a lot of ground to cover, but I didn't want to distract her either. As if sensing this, she glanced over her shoulder, her hair coming undone from the messy ponytail she had it in. She looked so sexy like that, face slightly flushed from the wine, wild hair, sweats and an old T-shirt. On particularly lonely nights, I envisioned her walking into my living room looking like that and plopping down onto the couch beside me, picking up where we left off like I hadn't broken her heart and sent her away. Maybe we'd do more than just talk, but ultimately, it was the idea of having her near that made the dream so spectacular. She hit a key on the computer.

"You can check the place out if you want while I finish this," she said. "There's a guest room over there." She pointed. "You can check out the basement. Your call."

"I'm fine."

She looked at her computer again, clicked a key, and spoke. After another minute, she glanced over at me again. "Is this the only leather you have?"

I pushed off the counter and walked over to her as she muted her side of the conversation. "Am I allowed near the sketches?"

"I guess you'll have to see them at some point."

I bit back a smile.

"Stop smiling." She scowled.

I lost the battle and laughed. "Sorry."

"Do you have any more leathers or not?"

"What color?"

"Blue. Preferably royal."

I reached for the book and looked at the spine. "I have another volume of blues. Do you want something attention-grabbing or tame? Is this for the hotel? Did you settle on a theme?"

"The leather is for a car project, but I just settled on a theme for the hotel as well. I'm waiting for Seth and Tommy to catch up."

I glanced at the screen to find both the guys staring at her expectantly and nodded toward it. She turned back, unmuting herself. "I'm so sorry guys," she said. "Anything?"

"I'm sending my file for the car over in the comments," Tommy said. Tessa clicked and grinned.

"Oh, I like the second one a lot."

I moved and sat on the other side of the couch so I had a better view but was still off camera. Tommy made a face.

"Who are you with?"

"None of your business," she snapped. "Focus."

"Okay. What do you like about the second one?"

"It actually looks like a rocket. Do we know for sure they're letting us choose the exterior color of the car too?"

"Positive," Seth said. "We can even take out parts if we want."

"They're crazy," Tessa said, clicking on something else on the computer. "I'm sending over my sketch of the seats. Bear in mind that it's super-duper rough, but I think it would look cool on bucket seats like these."

I watched her drag a file and drop it in the same little window. I couldn't make it out, but both guys made impressed faces and sounds.

"Damn, this is rough?" Seth chuckled.

The other guy grinned. "Fuck. I'd hate to upload one of my rough files. After seeing the Spring Collection dresses and now this?"

The three of them laughed and even though I couldn't see the file, I felt myself smile.

"Guys, this is serious. I'm freaking the fuck out. We have two presentations in a week. Let's move on to the hotel."

"Are we going with the Moroccan theme?" one of them asked.

"I don't know. I think that theme would be great in the lounge area," Tessa said. "The more I think about the furniture and ambiance, the more I think we should stick to sleek in the lobby. Something New York themed since the other cities have city themes. Whites and grays. Maybe incorporate something about Lady Liberty? We need to think about things that make people think New York."

"That'll be easy," one of the guys said. "You want to draw it or you want me to?"

Seth cleared his throat. "We'll do it. You look like you need a break."

"Is that your way of saying I look like shit?" she asked, scrubbing her face with her hands.

"No."

"You do look tired," the other guy offered.

She didn't just look tired. She looked worn out, which only got worse the longer the call ran. Eventually, despite their combined insanity, they reached an agreement on the theme and what each aspect of the design would entail. Personally, I thought they were way in over their heads, but if they could pull both projects off and they were using our fabrics, I'd be thrilled. When her meeting ended, she sighed and leaned back. I wanted to sit behind her, spread my legs so she was between them, and reach down to massage the knots out of her back. Something told me she would probably punch me if I tried.

"Can I see what you showed them?"

She lifted her gaze briefly and clicked on her computer. I moved to sit beside her on the floor, my left arm touching her right. Even that made my pulse spike. She opened a sketch of a car seat, which was already shaded in with the blue she was looking for. It was rich and colorful and made me think of the women in Colombia with their amazing fabrics and leathers and their refusal to cooperate with a man-owned company. I'd decided long ago that I wouldn't involve Camryn in any of that, but Tessa? I'd trust her with anything.

"I know where we can get your fabric."

"You don't have it?"

"Not the perfect one for this." Not in leather and definitely not in that rich royal blue.

"If it's that perfect, I'm surprised you haven't bought the entire company yet."

I felt my lips tug. "Not for lack of trying. It's owned by a Colombian woman who refuses to sell to a man."

This made her laugh. "You're kidding."

"Not kidding. Trust me, I've tried many times."

"Why not send a female employee?"

"I don't have one that fits the bill."

"Well, I can't go to Colombia," she said. "I have to finish this presentation by next week."

"She's in Miami right now," I said. "And I can set up a meeting, if she can't come up here, we can take one day, two tops. I can get you the swatches. You don't have to have the fabric for the presentation, you just need it in time for the actual manufacturing."

"Do you think she will go for that?"

"It can't hurt to reach out." With that, she nodded in agreement. We looked at each other for a long moment. The air seemed to shift between us. I put my hand over hers between us on the floor. "There's something else I want to talk to you about."

She licked her lips. It was that simple action that made me realize how much I longed for her. She made me long for things that hadn't even crossed my mind since she left, like leaning in and brushing my lips against hers. Would she let me or turn me away? Could we kiss and talk later? Could I stop at just one kiss? Doubtful. I'd waited too long to have her. I'd dreamed too often of her skin, her lips, her touch.

"We can't," she whispered, reading my thoughts.

"I'm desperate for you."

"You're married."

"Only on paper."

"You keep saying that."

"Because it's the truth and you know it."

"It doesn't make it mean any less."

I nodded my understanding. When it was the other way around and I thought she was with Cody Maverick, I hadn't wanted to be the Mariah in the situation either.

I changed directions.

"I went to see my dad yesterday."

"Oh?"

"It had been at least a year since I last saw him."

"How'd it go?"

"It went well. Strange, but well. We had a good talk."

"I'm glad." She gave me a small smile, her eyes closing. She looked so exhausted so I gambled and put an arm around her, pulling her against my side and fully expecting her to fight me. Instead, she laid her head on my chest and exhaled. My heart felt like it would pound straight out of my chest. "This doesn't mean anything."

To me, it meant everything. I held her in place when she tried to shimmy away. "Just, please, Tessa. Just this."

She stopped moving and yawned. "You can't just barge into our lives like a hurricane. I don't have a personal FEMA to take care of me and Miles when you decide you've had enough of us."

"You think I could ever get enough of you?"

I felt her stiffen. I wasn't going to take the words back. I knew what she was thinking. I could practically feel her thoughts punching me. I deserved it. I'd own up to it, but in the end, it wouldn't matter, because I was still going to get her.

"Do you really think I'd be that horrible of a father?" I heard myself whisper after a long, silent moment.

"I think you'd be an amazing father."

"I would never take him away from you, Tessa. I need you to believe that." I stroked her hair. "Everything I said the other day . . . I was angry, and while I think it'll take me a little while to fully get over my anger, that little boy . . ." I exhaled, shaking my head as I smiled against her head. "Being around him makes me upset that I've missed so many things."

"I recorded them," she whispered. I pulled back, cupping her face and tilting it so she'd look at me. "Every holiday, every birthday, every milestone. I know it isn't the same and it doesn't change the fact that I kept him from you, but I thought that someday you may want to see those things." When she blinked, tears rolled down her face. "I'm sorry that I'm so selfish, but he's my best friend. He's everything. I don't know what I'd do if I had to let go of him for weekends at a time."

I pulled her over to kiss the top of her head. "We'll figure it out."

I didn't bother mentioning that I wasn't planning to take him away for weekends at a time because I was going to do everything in my power to marry this girl. I'd have to work twice as hard to get out of the situation I was in, but I'd do it.

CHAPTER TWENTY

TESSA

WE FELL asleep on the floor, sitting upright. It wasn't until Rowan shifted beside me and lifted me into his arms that I realized it, and by then it was too late, he was already walking toward the rooms. I lifted an arm and pointed at the guest room I'd been using, and he headed that way. As he walked, I let myself revel in the way I felt in his strong arms. I closed my eyes and let myself dream of things I hadn't even contemplated before tonight. Him being around for Miles meant nothing in terms of our relationship. It didn't matter how tempting he was, we had a lot of work to do before I could let him back into my life in that way, assuming he wanted that. It wasn't as if he'd outright said that to me, but the way he looked at me said enough.

He set me on the bed and when I settled onto my side, he crawled in next to me.

"You're sleeping here?"

"Is that a problem?"

"Um . . ." My heart rattled. It was a problem because I actually wanted him to sleep here. "Don't you have an apartment nearby?"

"It's missing a lot of things."

I couldn't see him in the dark, but I turned toward him anyway. "Like furniture?"

"Like you."

"Rowan," I warned. I didn't like the way my pulse quickened.

"Tessa," he mimicked.

"You know, there are two other rooms available."

"You aren't in either of those rooms," he said, pausing. "Do you really want me to leave?"

No. That was the real answer. I didn't want him to leave and that was a problem. "I agreed to you seeing Miles. I'm not agreeing to you seeing me. It wouldn't work."

"That's where you're wrong."

"Do I need to keep reminding you that you're married to another woman?"

"No," he said softly. "Do I need to keep reminding you that the marriage is a façade? That the only woman I care about is lying next to me right now."

"Stop saying things like that," I whispered.

"I've been bottling things like that up for years."

"And you suddenly decided that you can open up and tell me them? Did you figure out that you bleed like the rest of us?"

"Yes."

I blinked. What was happening? "Even after these projects

are done with, we'll have to see each other and work together for Miles. Parenthood doesn't stop at end of business."

"You already said that and I'm ready for it."

"Good."

"It isn't my son I'm worried about. It's his mother. I don't know if I can have her in small doses," he said. "I don't think I want to try."

"I don't think I want to find out where this can lead if I don't go to sleep right now."

He reached for me, took a hold of my hand, and squeezed it. "Rest."

I nodded in the dark, slipped my hand from his, and turned over to face to opposite wall.

"Would you believe me if I told you that I've spent these last few years regretting every decision I made before you left?" he asked into the darkness.

"Considering who you married, yes."

"I could have married any random woman and I would still feel this way because she wasn't you."

His words hit me smack in the middle of my chest, spreading the warmth of a sunrise after a seemingly endless night. "Ro, go to sleep."

"Okay, but I need you to know that I'm not going anywhere."

For the first time in my life, I knew that to be true. I wasn't sure if it was because of the assurance Miles brought or because I could genuinely feel that he meant it, but I liked it.

THE SOUND of the shower woke me the next morning. I turned over and scooted into the space Rowan had vacated. The pillow smelled like him. I closed my eyes and breathed it in, waiting for the water to stop and for him to get out of the bathroom so I could use it. When the water turned off, I rolled back to my side, heart pounding as I waited.

There was something about knowing that he was fewer than twenty feet away from me, soaking wet and naked, that made me feel a bit unhinged, too hot in my own skin.

When he finally opened the door, I was half-relieved, half-disappointed that he was completely dressed in gray sweatpants and a black T-shirt. His hair was clearly wet and brushed back away from his face. His beard, which was so much sexier than I thought a beard had any right to be, had obviously just been trimmed.

Maybe that was what scared me about the whole thing with Miles. I wasn't sure how I'd handle Rowan coming into our lives and nitpicking at everything I'd built for my son. I got out of bed and grabbed my overnight bag on my way over to the bathroom. He moved out of the way slowly, as if his feet were dragging him in the opposite direction, but he really wanted to stay.

"I'm going to . . ." I started, pointing at the bathroom.

He cleared his throat. "Yeah, I'm going to get us breakfast. I'll be right back."

I darted into the bathroom, closed the door behind me, and leaned against it for a moment. I really needed to get a hold of myself in front of him, but after all of the things he said last night, I knew it wouldn't be that easy. It didn't change the fact that I needed to finish setting up my presentations and figure out how to introduce him to Miles. Really introduce him to Miles, unlike the other day. It wasn't as if he hadn't asked about his dad. His teacher had sent out a letter about a Father's Day breakfast the school was setting up and while I'd already enlisted Freddie with the task of going, I had to dodge questions from him about his real dad. Thankfully, he'd just started asking.

He'd only ever had me, so he didn't think it was abnormal until he was forced into social settings with people who had both.

The same went for grandparents and siblings and . . . hell, even pets. We took our cues from society in every aspect of our lives. I'd told Miles that not everyone had a father or mother or grandparents. It seemed to appease him, but only because Uncle Freddie was going to be there with him. It made me sad, not for him, but for so many kids out there who would be missing their father. It also made the guilt flare inside me because it was my fault that his wouldn't be going. I dried myself and dressed quickly, picking everything up as I went.

When I opened the door to the bedroom, the smell of bacon hit me, and my stomach once again, growled, reminding me that I hadn't been very good to it lately. I found Rowan in the kitchen, his back toward me as he flipped something in a pan.

"You're cooking?" I sat in front of one of the settings on the counter. "This is new."

The smile he flashed me over his shoulder made my pulse skitter. "Stick around, I'll show you all my new tricks."

"Hm." *Maybe I will,* I added silently as I watched him fix two plates, setting one in front of me and the other beside me. He brought a mug and placed it in front of me next.

"You still take it black like your soul, right?"

"Yeah." I smiled. "You still take yours as sweet as yours?"

He winked. "You know it."

I couldn't stop smiling as I ate. "This is really good."

"At your service."

"Miles would like the pancakes."

He was silent for a beat before asking, "What's his favorite food?"

"Depends. He'd probably say bacon."

Rowan chuckled. "A boy after my own heart."

"Yeah, hearts that bacon definitely doesn't help."

He kept chewing, but even after I looked away, I could feel his eyes on me. "What else does he like?"

"To eat?"

"Or do, or anything."

"He's obsessed with the sky," I continued. "He loves constellations and rockets and the idea of being an astronaut. He also loves tools, so if you leave any out, you can be sure he's going to take them and use them for something. He loves to read, ice cream, the park." I shrugged. "Stuff like that."

"How are you going to tell him about me?"

I was glad I'd finished eating and had put my fork down because otherwise I would've dropped it. "I don't know."

"But you are going to tell him."

I swiveled in my seat and faced him, brought my hand up to his face, and looked into those concerned blue eyes. "I'm going to tell him."

HE KISSED me when we said goodbye. It wasn't a long-lasting kiss, just a peck, but my lips were still warm from it. We drove back in separate cars. When I got home, I went straight to my bedroom and started unpacking. I'd dressed in what I called business-chic this morning, which was really just dark jeans, a plain button-down blouse, and flats, and then I headed into the office. The entire way, I moved on autopilot, too consumed with what I would tell Miles to pay much attention.

I'd given him my new phone number and saved his. I was specific in that he should only call me for things pertaining to Miles. Yes, the hopeless romantic in me wanted to get lost in the idea of love again, but I was also very aware that the last time I felt this way about this man, it ended in heartache. I'd definitely be careful this time, but I wasn't going to rule anything out. One thing I learned in the aftermath of our love was that my heart can crack, break into a million pieces, and shatter like glass, but it kept beating. In my case, it definitely kept beating, for Miles, for myself.

By the time I arrived at the office, I felt refreshed. As Seth, Tommy, Chloe, and I sat in the conference room waiting for Ryan Ford to join us, we all buzzed in anticipation. We rehearsed our presentation, presented it to Ryan. Once he gave us the thumbs-up, we called the car company and video chatted the presentation to them about our rocket concept car for Fashion Week. Then we called the boutique hotel and pitched our ideas. The whole time I gave the presentation and showed him our conceptual design, I wished I could turn around and look at Ryan's face. The man I was talking to looked so much like him, with the same dark brown eyes and dark hair, they even had the same little cleft on their chins. The man, Brody Ford, looked too much like Ryan to be anything other than family.

When we were finished, Brody smiled and thanked us. His attention seemed to be behind me, though, where Ryan sat. I moved out of the way and looked over there.

"What do you think?" Ryan asked.

"I think you're a son of a bitch and I'm going to have to pick you," Brody replied. "But you already knew this."

"I'll tell Donovan," Ryan said with a twinkle in his eye.

"Don't you dare," Brody warned. "Thank you for everything. You captured everything we're looking for. I'll expect the contract so we can start right away."

And then the video cut. We all looked at each other, stunned into complete silence.

I spoke first.

"He's your brother."

"What gave it away?"

"Why did we jump through hoops for this if you knew you were going to end up with the contract anyway?" I asked.

"I didn't know we'd end up with the contract," he said simply.

"Just because he's my brother doesn't mean I dictate his decisions."

There was another stretch of silence and then Seth clapped his hands and stood.

"I'm excited about this. I'm going to talk to the furniture company first and then call the car people to see when we can get the seats down here to start on that."

I nodded. "I'll finish with the fabrics that we picked for the hotel. I'm thinking maybe we can upholster the walls in a pretty ivory. Maybe add buttons for texture."

"Like a backboard?" Chloe asked, jotting it all down on her clipboard.

"Yeah, sort of like that."

Ryan stood. "I like where all of this is going. Tessa, a word?"

"Sure."

I followed him out of the conference room and into the hall, where he stopped and turned to me.

"What's going on with the fabrics?"

"I narrowed down the hotel fabrics for the lobby," I said, because that had been the easy part. "I have ideas for the lounge area as well and now that we got the job, I think it should be easy to figure out the rest of the layouts."

"Right. What about the leather for the car seats?"

"That . . . well, Rowan Hawthorne seems to think he has the perfect leather for it, as well as other colorful fabrics, but they're owned by another company."

"Tell him to get them."

"That's the problem." I glanced away, hoping to hide the cringe I felt coming on. "The lady won't sell to a man-owned and operated company."

Ryan looked at me like I was growing tentacles. "What do you mean?"

"Exactly that. She won't sell Rowan her fabrics."

"That's the stupidest thing I've ever heard." He frowned. "She's losing business. All textiles companies are owned by men."

"Not true, actually," I said.

"Well, most of them are."

"Well, the one that seems to matter in this conversation is not only owned by a woman but also owned by a woman who doesn't want to work with men."

He raised an eyebrow. "Why don't you speak to her? You're a woman and the director of your department. That has to count for something."

"I'll see what I can do." I moved to walk back into the conference room.

"I want to see this fabric," Ryan said as he walked into his office. "Have it on my desk by Monday. I know this is your project, but all of our reputations are riding on this. If it doesn't live up to the hype, we're moving on."

CHAPTER TWENTY-ONE

ROWAN

UNLIKE THE PREVIOUS times I'd been there, the main door to Tessa's building was unlocked and I was able to walk right in. Also, unlike previous times, there was no Freddie or Celia in sight as I stood outside of Tessa's door, knocking for the third time. I hadn't told her I was coming over, though, in my defense, I'd called and texted, but she hadn't responded. I lifted my hand one more time with the intention of knocking a little louder when the door swung open. Tessa was on the other side of it, wearing the shortest blue shirt I'd ever seen—she may as well have been wearing a bra—and gray sweats that hung low on her hips. All Yale. All sexy. All *mine*. Nothing made my blood boil like the sight of her. She pushed her hair, which was wet, out of her face and looked at me.

"What are you doing here?"

"Mommyyyyyyyyyy," a little voice called out.

"Sorry. It's bedtime." She blew out a long breath and turned around, leaving me standing in the doorway. I took the opportunity and stepped inside, closing and locking the door behind me. Miles ran around the corner and came to a dead stop when he saw me. He was wearing Beast pajamas from *Beauty and the Beast*, his blue eyes wide on mine. His dark hair was perfectly brushed to the side.

"I said in a minute, Miles," Tessa said, walking over to him. He lifted his arms as she lowered hers to pick him up. It was all done on autopilot, the way you perform secondary things like tying your shoes.

"You took too long." He wrapped his arms around her and continued to look at me over her shoulder.

I'd never seen a toddler glare, but I was pretty sure that was what he was doing. I fought a laugh as they went into what I assumed was his room. I didn't follow, not because I didn't want to but because it was obvious that I was interrupting some sort of ritual they had and he wasn't happy about it.

While I waited, I took my phone out and googled the best way to introduce yourself to your girlfriend's child. It wasn't exactly what I was doing, but I couldn't even think of a way to phrase the reality of this situation. The first link took me to a message board where the women talked about dating after a divorce. Each response made me a little more baffled and upset than the last. Most of them seemed to be happily dating, not even a mention of the ex-husband in the picture. I hated it. I reminded myself once again that this wasn't an ordinary case and kept scrolling.

"You can come back," Tessa called out.

I put my phone away and the pressure in my chest seemed to lessen as I followed the sound of her voice. I stopped at the door and looked around. There were scattered toys on the floor, the walls were blue and had silver constellations and stars painted on them. The windowsill had an outline of a rocket surrounding it. Even the bed looked like a spacecraft. On the left of it was a small bookshelf, a desk, and a dresser with a basket of clothes on it. Tessa covered Miles, who still had his eyes on me, and walked over to the bookshelf.

"What book do we want today?" she asked.

"*Giving Tree.*"

She sighed. "Really?"

He nodded, a little smile on his face as he looked at her back. Even in my limited experience with things like these, I could feel the love he felt for his mother. It was pure and wholesome and impossible to escape. It was in the way he watched her and in the way he looked at me as if he didn't want me anywhere near her. Tessa took the book from the shelf and flipped to the first page as she sat on a child-sized blue couch beside his bed. I leaned against the doorframe and listened to her as she read the story to him. He turned over on his side so he could look at the pictures, smiling every time she read something in a different voice. Everything about her enthralled me. The way she tucked her hair behind her ear each time it fell in front of the pages. The way she made her voice loud or soft, depending on what character was speaking. The way she glanced up and touched his hair every so often once she turned the page. I had never deserved this woman. Not when we were kids, not when we were teenagers, not four years ago, and certainly not now. I'd never done anything to deserve her attention or her love, yet, she gave it to me continuously without asking for anything in return.

She'd given me a son and not asked for anything in exchange. Seeing her with him, the life she'd created for him without my help, made me realize she'd never needed me. She'd spent so much of her life worrying about being held back because she needed a man in her life, and she'd proven time and time again that she didn't. It was refreshing to see and I never would have thought that before this moment. Maybe it was because my mother always needed my father and I had hated that for her. It was the reason the affair and the divorce had been so hard on her. She'd told me as much recently. Even Camryn, with all her traveling and doing what she wanted always revolved everything around a man, whether it be me, Wall Street guy, to the random guy she picked up.

Standing there, I acknowledged more than just how the women in my life depended on me. I admitted, if only to myself, that how I felt watching Tessa and Miles must have been how my father felt about Mariah and the son they had together. That how I felt about Camryn was how my father felt about my mother. Sure, circumstances were different. I wasn't him. I understood that. It didn't change the fact that on paper our situations were eerily similar.

By the time she finished reading the book, I could hear the tears in her voice. It was a damn powerful story. She closed it, wiped her face, and kissed Miles on the forehead, her fingers running through his hair softly.

"I love you."

"I love you, Mommy."

With that, she flicked on the nightlight, which shot a reflection of stars up on the ceiling, grabbed the basket of clothes, and shooed me out. I took a few steps back, my eyes riveted to her every movement as she joined me. Raw emotions rioted inside me, reminding me of all of the things I didn't even know I wanted until just the other day. Except Tessa. I'd always wanted her, but this life? This settled down, familiar life? When had I ever dreamed of that? Never. Not until I knew the possibility was real and damn it, I wanted it more than I'd ever wanted anything. I followed her to the living room, where she dumped the basket on a couch and began to sort out clothes and fold them. I could feel her exhaustion even from where I stood, so instead of sitting on the opposite couch, I sat beside her on the center ottoman and joined her. Her hands stopped moving, her gaze jumping to mine.

"Let me do this," I said. She scanned my face, seemingly looking for some unknown reason as to why I'd want to fold Miles's clothes. Truth was, I hated folding clothes, but having my son's clothes in my hands made me feel closer to him even though he had no idea what I was to him. After a moment, she let go of the shirt in her hands and let me take over.

"You're so good with him," I said, my voice a hoarse whisper. I glanced up at her. "I'm in awe of you."

She looked stricken for a beat before she cleared her throat. "Thanks. Do you want something to drink? Wine? Hot chocolate? Beer? Water? Passion fruit juice?"

"Wine will do." I felt myself smile. She stood and walked over to the kitchen. I continued folding clothes. There were two soccer uniforms, one baseball uniform, a lot of NASA related apparel, one Yankees T-shirt, one Mets T-shirt, one Cubs T-shirt. I stopped folding. Was she letting my kid root for all of these teams? I looked up as she approached and took the glass of wine from her hand.

"Are you letting him root for three different baseball teams?"

She sat across from me, on the empty couch. "Who cares? You don't even like baseball."

"I respect it."

"You think it's boring." She took a sip of wine and heat spread inside me at the sight of her parted lips, the way her throat moved as she swallowed. God, I wanted her. I wanted to lick the wine from her lips and drag my way down the rest of her body. She shot me a look. "Stop looking at me like that."

"Like what?"

"You know like what," she said, glancing down the hallway. "I know what you look like when you're turned on."

Fuck. And I was. So turned on. I shook the T-shirts in my hand. "Can we go back to the issue at hand?"

"He likes the colors. He's obsessed with blues. Those are three different hues of blue." She shrugged and then rolled her eyes. "What are you doing here anyway? How did this even happen?"

"What part?"

"You coming over, folding clothes, and drinking my wine."

"You offered your wine. I offered to fold clothes."

"But why are you here?"

"I called you. You didn't answer."

Amusement lit in her eyes. Her lips moved into a slight smile. "I forgot. You chase down women who don't call you back. How's that working out for you?"

"As it turns out, I seem to only chase one woman." I searched her eyes. "I'm still working on it."

"Building a textiles empire, trying to get into your son's life, and chasing this woman? However will you manage it all?"

"I'll gladly drop the first one if it means getting the other two." I meant it. I could see that she didn't completely believe me, but that was okay. I would take the time to make her believe me. She cleared her throat and set her glass on the side table. "When did you bring him? For the games," I asked.

"In the spring when Prim told me about the promotion. We flew over and went to a Yankees game, but Miles wanted a shirt from both teams, and then we went to the Mets game, where he wanted both teams as well."

I gaped at her. "That's unacceptable."

She laughed. "Sam got him the Cubs shirt last Christmas."

Of course. Sam. I tried not to let that pierce my heart. My brother had been there for Miles and I wouldn't let my jealousy cloud that. I hadn't had a face-to-face conversation with him about all of this yet, but we'd spoken a few times over the phone, and I was at peace with it. I didn't believe him when he said he didn't know, but I was learning that moving past things and seeing the bigger picture was more important than being caught up in the little things.

"You look tired."

"Thanks." She shot me a dirty look.

"Come here." I set the clothes down and lifted one of her feet onto my lap and then the other. She let me, probably because she was so tired. She closed her eyes and leaned her head back as I started to massage her foot. "Did you speak to Ryan about the fabric?"

"He said I need to get the fabrics by Monday."

My hands stopped moving. "It's Thursday."

"Which gives you four days to get me the fabric." She lifted her head and looked at me. "Aren't you Mr. Go-Getter?"

"I told you I need help getting this done."

"What's the status on the meeting?"

"I emailed that to Chloe. She's willing to meet us this Saturday in Miami and show you the fabrics in person. It's a weekend, but she's limited on days."

"That's fine."

"Why don't we make a weekend out of it?" I suggested. Tessa's eyes widened.

"I just came back from a trip."

"That was a mental health slash work trip. That doesn't

count. I mean a quick getaway, just the two of us. We can get on the same page about Miles and celebrate your birthday." I smiled at the look on her face. Clearly, she didn't think I would remember. "When was the last time you took a birthday trip?"

She laughed. "Probably never."

"We can go down to Miami." I raised an eyebrow.

"When would this trip take place? Assuming I say yes."

"Tomorrow. We can come back on Sunday."

"What?" She sat upright. "I can't just take an impromptu trip! We have a lot of ground to cover on parenting one-oh-one."

"We'll cover it on the trip. Do you want to bring Miles?"

"You're serious." She blinked slowly, openly gaping at me.

"Of course, I'm serious."

"I'm not taking Miles to Miami. I'd take him to Orlando, but what's he going to do in Miami?"

I shrugged. Hell if I knew. I'd been there once for a bachelor party and barely remembered my time there. "We can also find out if the fabrics company would be open to a meeting while we're there."

"Hm." She studied me for a long moment.

"Your mom and Joan are still here. Freddie and Celia—"

"Freddie's out of town for work, but yes," she said, knowing where I was going with this. "I'd be able to leave Miles with them for a day or two. Preferably one, though."

"A twenty-four-hour trip?"

She sighed heavily. "It can be longer, but not much longer."

I grinned, fishing my phone out to book the trip.

"Oh my god. I can't believe I'm agreeing to this. All I wanted for my birthday was to get my hair and nails done and you're over here springing this on me."

"How soon can you get your hair and nails done?"

"Tomorrow morning if I don't go to the office but the daycare isn't open tomorrow because—"

"I'll watch Miles. If you let me," I said, swallowing the lump that seemed to keep coming back. She looked startled. I waited for her to say no, to tell me I didn't have a clue what I was doing and wouldn't know how to handle him. Instead, she lowered her feet slowly and sat up, closer to me.

"You'd have to be here early."

"I would stay the night if you'd let me."

"We aren't ready for that." Her eyes widened. "It's too soon for Miles. I've never had a man . . ." She let the words hang, but I caught her drift.

"We don't have to share a bed. I can take the couch."

"You don't have clothes here. You'd have to pack too. Don't you need to be at work tomorrow? At what time would we leave?"

"I'll work from here. I'll go home, get clothes, and come right back." I waited, smiling when I realized I really had her. "Keep throwing around excuses. I'll keep finding a way around them."

"Believe me, I know you will." She shot me a pointed look. "Fine. Go home and come back."

She stood and walked into the kitchen, finishing her wine on the way over there, and then returned with a set of keys. I stood in front of her, loving the way I towered over her. Squashing the urge to pull her into my arms and kiss her, hold her, anything to have her near. She shot me a pointed look, seemingly reading my thoughts, and handed me the keys. "I want these back. You haven't earned them. But I am way too tired to wait up for you."

I held her fingers between mine as I took the keys from her and leaned in. Her breath caught. I placed my forehead against hers, closed my eyes, and breathed out. She did the same.

"Thank you."

"The keys are temporary," she whispered.

"Temporary has potential to become permanent."

With that, I pulled away and went home. I jogged back,

hoping it would help kill the adrenaline running through me. I knew I'd have to take a nice, cold shower when I got there. And jerk off. There was no way I'd survive the night without both. I hadn't felt this way in a long while, and a part of me welcomed it. I wasn't broken after all. As I neared my place, I slowed my jog and glowered at the person standing by my stoop.

"What are you doing here?"

"Waiting for you, obviously," Camryn said, taking a step toward me.

"Unless you came over to tell me you signed the papers, I want nothing to do with you," I said. "From now on, anything you need to tell me needs to be said through your lawyer. I'm not fucking kidding about that."

She balked. "What? You can't just order me away like that."

"I just did." I brushed past her, taking the steps quickly. She grabbed my arm.

"Tessa's back." Her words made cold dread seep through me. "You aren't the only one who knows to hire a PI in the middle of a divorce."

I kept my eyes on my door because I didn't want her to know how uncomfortable this made me and I waited for her to tell me she knew about Miles. My stomach churned at the thought of a random guy with a camera following my kid around.

"What's your point?" I made myself sound bored.

"My point is that if you think I'm going to sign those papers so you can run off into the sunset with her, you have another think coming," she said. "Your mom is on my side. If you have any doubts about it, you should try calling her sometime."

"What the fuck does my mother have to do with this?" I yanked my arm away and turned around to cut her with my glare.

"I'm just letting you know that I have more people on my side than you have on yours," she said, raising an eyebrow. "I'm sure that if I call your father tomorrow I'll have him on my side as well. And your grandmother, what will she think when she finds out you're trying to get a divorce before the contract is up?"

"The contract is almost up, so you can go right ahead and call the entire fucking world for all I care. This divorce is happening."

I turned around and this time, I unlocked my door and shut it right in her face.

CHAPTER TWENTY-TWO

TESSA

I COULDN'T REMEMBER the last time I fell into such a deep slumber, but when I woke, I was startled to see the sun was up and the clock on my nightstand said it was seven. I shot out of bed and ran out of my room to wake Miles up, stopping dead in my tracks at the sound of chatter coming from the kitchen. Miles laughed. I frowned, making my way down the hallway before stopping again at the threshold. Rowan's back was turned toward me and Miles was sitting on one of the tall barstools, the ones I never let him sit on unless I was beside him because I feared he'd fall and hurt himself. Yes, I was that paranoid.

"Mommy," he said cheerfully when he spotted me and suddenly both pairs of deep blue eyes were looking in my direction. I strode over to Miles, gave him a hug, and kept him in the center of the chair. "Careful, buddy."

"I'm not gonna fall."

"You might." I raised an eyebrow. He'd changed out of his pajamas and was wearing his favorite sweatpants and NASA T-shirt. "You dressed yourself?"

"Rowan helped."

I smiled at the way he carefully pronounced his name. I looked over at Rowan, who was plating the pancakes he'd made. He walked over, set one of the plates in front of Miles, leaned in, and kissed my forehead before going back for the other plates.

"Thank you," I said as he set one in front of me before wrapping an arm around my waist. Goose bumps spread over my skin at the feel of his hand on me.

"You don't have to thank me," he said against my hair. "I made chocolate chip. You want coffee?"

"Yes, but I'll eat after I shower. I'll be quick."

"I was able to secure a meeting with the owner of the fabric company for tomorrow afternoon," he said. "Our flight is tonight. All of the information is in your personal email, which I got from Chloe."

My mouth dropped. He winked as I ducked away from him and ran back to my room, heading straight to the en-suite bathroom, trying not to let the familiarity of our exchange in the kitchen get to me. I showered and dressed quickly, and once I was finished, I packed a bag. I didn't want to leave Miles behind again, especially because I'd just been gone for two days, but Celia and Mom would keep him busy. What I was more concerned about was who was going to keep me too busy to think about Rowan. On that note, I picked up the phone and called my mom, explaining that I was going to Miami with Rowan for work.

I left out the birthday celebration part because I knew she'd make a big deal of it.

"With Rowan, huh?"

"Yes." I held my breath in anticipation. Her tone told me she would ask a million questions. "We're leaving tonight, but I'll be back Sunday by nine in the morning."

"Hm. Why the rush?"

"Because it's a work trip," I said. "Celia already knows about it and said she'd watch Miles, but I wanted to let you know anyway. I'm going to go to the salon right now."

"Isn't Celia in a meeting right now?"

"She is."

"Who's watching Miles while you go to the salon? Are you taking him?"

"No." I swallowed. "Rowan is here. He's going to watch him."

"Interesting," she said, then spoke to my grandmother. "Mom, Tessa is letting Rowan stay with Miles. Wouldn't you say that's interesting?"

"Mom."

"What? Excuse me if pieces of the puzzle are finally coming together."

I squeezed my eyes shut. "Mom."

"It's fine, Tessa. I just don't understand why you'd feel the need to keep that from me all this time."

"Because there was no point in addressing it. What good would it have done if you'd known he was Miles's father?"

"I would have called Mildred and Alistair and told them what a son of a bitch their son was."

"Rowan didn't know."

She stayed quiet for a beat. "Jesus, Tessa."

"I know. I'm sorry I kept it from you and Freddie and Dad and Rowan and Sam, but I didn't want anyone to know. Least of all Mildred."

"I understand," she said in a soft voice. "But I'm not Mildred."

"I know. I'm sorry." I slumped down on the edge of the bed.

"I forgive you," she said after a moment. "I'll be there in a few hours."

"That's fine. Take your time. I just wanted to fill you in on the details." I walked back into the kitchen where Rowan was loading the dishes into the dishwasher. Miles had moved from the barstool to the couch and was watching Mickey.

"Does your father know?"

"Not yet."

Rowan chose that very moment to switch off the water and close the dishwasher and turn his attention to me.

"No and no," I said to Mom. "I will soon."

"He's coming next week."

My eyes widened. "Why?"

"Your birthday," she said in a voice that hinted she thought I may be losing my mind. I just might be. Still. The thought of having to tell my dad all of this made me break out in a sweat. "He gets here Thursday," she added.

"You have a week to figure out what to say," Grandma Joan said in the background.

"I can't believe you have me on speaker phone."

"So?"

"Mom. Are you in an Uber?"

She paused again. "Why?"

"Because you just told your Uber driver my entire life story. Seriously?"

"Who cares?" Grandma added. "Edmund, is this the worst story you've heard?"

"Oh my god." I covered my face. "I'm hanging up now." And I did. Rowan's chuckle made me look up at him. "It isn't funny."

"It's sort of funny," he said, walking over to me. He stood

close, too close. I glanced briefly at Miles, who had his eyes set on Minnie Mouse. When I looked back up at Rowan, he had moved farther into my personal space.

"You're in my personal space."

His grin widened. "Does it bother you?"

No. Not at all.

"Yes."

"Hm. Maybe I shouldn't kiss you then," he whispered.

I shook my head. "Definitely not."

"You sure?" He brought his hand up to my face.

I nodded, lips slightly parting, heart hammering.

"I really want to." The low rasp in his voice sent a shiver down my spine. Between that and the way his eyes were piercing into mine, I felt I might lose my balance right there. He seemed to know this, because he ducked his face toward mine, put his forehead against mine, and breathed out. "I really, really want to."

That rasp vibrated through me once more. I opened my eyes and looked at him. "You haven't earned that."

"I will." He had a way of saying things that made me believe them and this was no different.

THE LADIES at the salon did my hair and nails at the same time. It was glorious. I walked out of there with a little kick in my step and headed to the juice bar across the street. I'd put in an order for three juices—one for me, one for Rowan, and one for Miles and was waiting for my number to be called when Camryn showed up. I swore the hairs on the back of my neck stood as she neared me. I didn't even need to fully look at her to know she was there, but I looked anyway.

"Tessa," she said in a cheerful voice. "What an interesting surprise! I thought you were living in Paris."

I forced a smile on my face. "Not anymore." I faced the counter again, clutching the receipt in my hand, willing my number to be called.

"Have you seen Samson or anyone?"

"Why?" I looked over at her again. She shrugged nonchalantly, bringing her left hand up to fix her hair in a motion that made it impossible for me to miss the huge rock on her finger. She smiled.

"Pretty right?"

I shrugged and once again looked at the counter.

"Ro thought it would be too big for my finger, but I'm glad he went with it," she continued. "We've been having some issues lately, but nothing we won't move past. Marriage is, like, so much work. I mean, definitely not for the weak."

I nodded as if I was disinterested, but she knew I was listening.

"It would be a shame to let anyone come between us," she said. "I mean that it would be devastating for sure. His mom is still heartbroken with everything that happened in her own marriage. She'd be so sad if Rowan and I split up."

"Why are you telling me this?" I finally looked at her again. "Do you not have friends to rant to? Because I'm telling you right now I don't give a shit about your marital issues or your husband or his mother."

Her eyes widened. "Oh. I was just making conversation."

"Well, make conversation with someone who actually cares to hear your stupid, insignificant, childish shit."

My number was called. Finally. I smiled wide at the barista as I stepped forward and grabbed my cup holder. I brushed past Camryn and walked out of there reeling. Thankfully, I made it back to my building without shaking too hard and dropping the juices. When I got inside the apartment, Rowan had changed into jeans and a polo and was on the floor with Miles building a smaller telescope Dad had sent him for Christmas and I still hadn't gotten around to building. I set the cup holder down, handed them their juices, giving Miles a quick kiss in the process, and picked mine up. Rowan's eyes were on me the entire time. I didn't need to look directly at his face to know that. Because I felt them with every step I took, even as I went over to the refrigerator to hide my face in it and hopefully cool off.

"Let's finish this in a bit," Rowan said. "Why don't you go grab those rockets you wanted to show me?"

Miles ran off, juice in hand, and Rowan came up to me. I tried busying myself with the contents of the refrigerator.

"What's wrong?"

"Nothing."

"Your hair looks beautiful." He pulled a curl and wrapped it around his finger.

"Thanks."

He stepped behind me, wrapping an arm around my middle, and buried his face into my neck. I inhaled sharply, closing my eyes.

"Smells good too."

"Thanks." My voice sounded breathy. I needed him to get out of my space. "Rowan."

"I know. Let you go, get out of your space, don't kiss you, just be cordial for the sake of the son we share together," he murmured against me. "I'm trying, but it's so damn hard."

I let myself revel in that. It was so damn hard.

Then the memory of seeing Camryn came rushing back, and it stopped being so damn hard. I opened my eyes and moved my shoulders, forcing him to take a step back.

"I need to make sure everything's ready for Miles."

With that, I left the kitchen.

CHAPTER TWENTY-THREE

ROWAN

SHE WAS BEING DISTANT. I couldn't figure out what I'd done or said, but there had to have been something. Before she left the house, she'd looked happy. She said goodbye to Miles, received a lecture from both her mother and Joan, and as soon as the door closed behind us, she started treating me like a stranger. The cab ride was silent and when we got onto the plane, she picked up that stupid *US Weekly* magazine and hadn't so much as looked in my direction. I wanted to rip it from her hands and make her say more than just a few words to me.

"Why are you mad?"

"Who says I'm mad?" She turned the page, folded the magazine over, and lifted her feet under her, pointing her knees in the other direction.

"I know you're mad."

She glanced up at me briefly. "I'm not mad, I'm compartmentalizing."

I wanted to call bullshit, but I'd said those words to her in the past. They weren't a lie. I'd learned at a young age to compartmentalize things. It was the only way not to get caught up in my own turmoil about things going on at home. These last few years had taught me a lot and one of those lessons was that I needed to let others know how I felt. Seeing my brother go through his treatments and not knowing whether or not they'd work had taught me that. I decided to stay quiet. I didn't want to get into an argument on an airplane. I barely had room to move, let alone toss all of my emotions out there.

The minute we stepped outside of the airport and were hit with a wave of humidity, we started peeling off layers. I knew it would be hot, but damn.

"It's like a furnace." She picked up her hair and wound it into a bun.

"Can't argue there. We should take our things to the hotel and go get something to eat. I'm starving."

"Me too."

I rented us a car, plugged the hotel address into the GPS, and we set off toward the beach.

"We're meeting with Natasha, the owner of Medellin Fabrics, tomorrow," I said. "It's in an area called Doral. I should probably map that tonight so we don't waste too much time in the morning."

"That's fine."

I glanced over at her. She was looking out the window, staring into the bumper-to-bumper traffic, clearly holding a grudge over something she couldn't even address directly.

"Last time I was here I was in college," she said after a quiet moment. "Came with a group of friends. I would recommend places I visited, but I was drunk the whole time and don't actually remember the name of any of them."

"Sounds like a fun trip."

"So much fun."

I kept my eyes fixed on the city as we made our way to Miami Beach, which took over an hour instead of the thirty minutes the GPS had first quoted. Tessa called Miles and spoke to him for a while as we sat in traffic, telling him to behave and be good, and that she missed him. I wished I could reach over and take the phone and tell him I missed him and would see him soon as well. More than anything, I wished he'd actually say all those things to me the way he said them to her. One day at a time, I reminded myself. I couldn't expect to make huge strides just in one day of babysitting. Maybe I could take him to the Yankees season opener or a Giants game when football season started. I wondered if he'd like hockey. I had to ask Tessa about the sports he participated in. Was he any good? Did she need me to take him for her? I'd go anyway. I'd go to every single thing I'd missed out on thus far.

CHAPTER TWENTY-FOUR

TESSA

MIAMI WAS HOT. That was what I was chalking up this sudden warmth curling inside of me to as I watched a shirtless Rowan pace our hotel suite. He'd been on the phone for thirty minutes, talking to someone back in New York, and while I would have loved to say I was just being nosey, listening in on his conversation, the truth was that I couldn't stop staring. He'd mentioned he hadn't been going up state as often as he'd liked, therefore, not rowing, but his body was insane. Maybe it was an athlete thing. Maybe their bodies just stayed intact while the rest of us went to shit if we didn't work out twenty-four-seven, which .

. . who had time for that? But damn, the way the planes of his back stretched and his stomach remained flat and cut, and his arms . . . and his broad shoulders . . . and just everything. I made myself look away. He exhaled heavily as he hung up the phone and tossed it onto the bed beside me. The suite had one bedroom, one large living room, and a small kitchen. He said he'd take the couch if I insisted, which I had. Him sleeping beside me would lead to very, very bad things. Bad things that would probably end in mind-blowing orgasms . . . plural.

"Everything okay?"

"I leave for one day and everyone decides that they can't handle simple shit," he said, running a hand through his hair. "How hard can it be to follow directions? They're fucking written in our contract. The delivery address is on the goddamn box. I swear to god . . ." He exhaled again, pacing. "And to top it off, the delivery was supposed to be made yesterday, and they ran late because they couldn't find the box to begin with. I just—"

"Ro."

He stopped pacing and turned to me, still looking troubled.

"Can you stop worrying about the company for two seconds?" I asked. "You're in a gorgeous suite in Miami. I'm sure Sam can take care of whatever mishap happened. It's after work hours on a Friday. Go downstairs and have a drink, go to a club, do something that has nothing to do with work for five minutes."

My words seemed to sink in slowly, but I could see when they hit him because his blue eyes glimmered with something much darker than amusement and deeper than lust, something that had the power to draw me in and keep me forever if I let him. He strode toward me, making me incredibly aware that I was sitting in bed wearing nothing more than a plush white robe and a string bikini beneath. He stood beside me. Close, but not close enough. I needed him to stay at a distance. I was still reeling from seeing Camryn and everything she said. I didn't believe her, I knew better than that. Rowan may have his faults, but he had never once lied to me.

"You think I'm going to go downstairs and have a drink, go to a club, or do something else without you?"

"It doesn't matter to me." I shrugged. "I'm perfectly content—"

He sat beside me. I sat up and crossed my legs, bunching the material of the robe between my legs. The robe opened to expose my bikini top. His gaze landed there automatically. I kept my eyes on his throat, the way it moved when he swallowed thickly. His hand moved to my lap, and then my arm. His eyes met mine.

"Whatever you're doing, I'm doing," he said. The way he looked at me made me want to believe he meant more than in just that moment. I couldn't trust myself to believe that.

"I saw Camryn today."

He took his hand back and closed it into a fist over his bent leg. "Where?"

"The juice bar."

"Why didn't you tell me when you got home?"

"I was compartmentalizing." It was the second time I'd used that on him and with the way his expression seemed to fall a bit, I almost wished I hadn't. "She said you're having marital issues, but that this too shall pass. Marriage is hard. I believe those were her exact words."

"Marital issues." He let out a forced chuckle. "I served her divorce papers over a month ago. She hasn't signed them, but she knows it's inevitable. We aren't . . ." He exhaled, closing his eyes briefly. He pinned me with them when he opened them once more. "We are not together. We will never be together. I'm not saying this to you as a kid who's in high school or fresh out of college, Tessa. I'm saying this to you as a man who would give up his left arm to be with you."

My throat tightened. "What are you saying?"

He slid off the bed and knelt beside me, putting his hand up like an offering. I placed mine in his and tilted slightly to face him, heart pounding, waiting.

"I'm saying that I can't take back the last four years of my life, but that doesn't mean I can't change the way things will be going forward," he said. "I'm saying that I want to be in your life and Miles's life, not just as a co-parent, but as more if you'll have me."

"Rowan." I felt the tears building in my eyes before I could stop them.

"I love you, Tessa Monte. I bleed for you."

I closed my eyes. I had to because I couldn't bear to see the raw look in his eyes. Tears slid down my face. How long had I wanted to hear those words from him? My entire life. There hadn't been a single moment in which this hadn't been a dream of mine and it had just become a reality. The man I had thought was emotionless had proven me wrong and I couldn't even keep my eyes open long enough to acknowledge the words and say them back.

"I know you probably don't love me anymore or that you can't say the words back. I fucked up. I know I did, but I don't want to spend another moment in your presence without letting you know how I feel." He brought my hands up to his lips and kissed one and then the other. I opened my eyes, took my hands from him, and wiped my tears.

"Silly, stupid man," I whispered. "You think love is something that fades with time?"

"I don't know a thing about love. I only know what I feel for you." His lips twitched slightly. "You still love me?"

"I told you I loved you before and it changed nothing then. What makes you think it'll change something now?"

"The time that passed, the things that have happened, the son you gave birth to," he said. "Want more?"

"You still have Camryn. We can move mountains all day, but

as long as we have that cloud above us, we'll never find enough light to grow."

"I'm trying to get rid of her, I swear it."

"Try harder."

"I will."

"Good."

"Whatever she told you is a lie," he said. "I'm not going to sit here and promise you that things will be perfect. I travel a lot and your job is demanding, but it'll be better than it would have been four years ago, I can promise you that. I wasn't ready before, but I'm ready for you now if you'll have me."

"And Miles," I said.

"And Miles." His lips moved into a small smile that faltered before it fully formed. "What if I put too much pressure on Miles and he grows to resent me? What if—"

I reached out and ran my fingers through his soft hair. He shut his mouth and closed his eyes, taking a long, deep breath.

"You are more than that," I said. "You are more than your stupid money and your company. More than your last name and your reputation. You are more, Rowan Hawthorne, and Miles will see that."

A smirk tugged at his lips as he opened his eyes. "I don't think he likes me. I mean, he likes me when you aren't around, but the moment you step into the room, he looks at me like I'm trying to move in on his woman. I'll admit that it makes me kind of proud, but since I *am* trying to move in on his woman, I kind of need him on board."

I laughed. "He's very protective of me."

"I noticed."

"But he likes you. I promise."

"Good." He smiled up at me. "You want to go to that pool party or would you rather me order room service and skip it?" I tugged on his hair, and he bit his bottom lip and let out a little growl, his expression heating. "You may want to reconsider the things you're doing to me while you're sitting on a bed, barely clothed, with that expression on your face."

"I could say the same thing to you."

He let out a grating chuckle. "Don't go offering things like that to a starving man."

I tugged his hair harder, motioning him up to me. He shifted, coming face to face with me and then following me as I lay back onto the bed.

"You're gonna have to take the lead here," he whispered as he braced his hands on either side of me.

I wrapped my arms around the back of his neck, pulling him closer until the tips of our noses were touching.

"I don't want to push too far."

"You aren't pushing," I whispered against his lips. "I'm pulling."

It was all he needed before he brought his mouth to mine, licking the seam of my lips slowly, nipping the length of my bottom lip as I angled my head, urging him to give me more. His lips were soft against mine, his tongue moving slowly alongside mine in an unrushed kiss that spread like fire through my veins. His hand slid down the length of my body to the loose knot holding my robe closed. The fabric fell open and he pulled back, eyes hazy as he moved to straddle my legs and set me up so he could slide the fabric off my shoulders and pull it free. Bringing his hand back, he caressed the side of my face, the tops of my breasts, the slopes of my hips.

"I pictured you every night," he whispered, following the trail his hand made over me with his eyes. "Yet, no amount of imagination could come close to reality."

He moved off me, but his hand continued to make its way down my stomach, stopping just above the line of my bikini bottom. He hadn't even really touched me yet and I couldn't seem to catch my breath. The anticipation was akin to torture.

"Rowan."

"Give me a moment, Sprite."

"A moment for what?" I gasped. He brought both hands to the tops of my thighs, squeezing, kneading. I arched. "Rowan, please."

"In a moment."

"I think I'm going to die," I said, my voice a pant. He chuckled.

"If you don't give me a moment, I'm going to explode and this will be no fun."

He said it at the same moment that his thumbs swept up my inner thighs, stealing whatever protest I was about to make. I groaned and watched without taking a single breath as he leaned forward, bit the tail of the bow on my hip, and pulled back until the knot gave way. He held my gaze, heated and full of promises, as he repeated the move on the other side.

Then he reached up and untied the top as well—this time with fingers instead of teeth—and tossed them both aside to join my discarded robe and effectively leave me stark naked beneath him. Leaning forward, he placed a kiss on either side of my jaw, dragging his mouth down to my chest, dropping open-mouthed kisses as he made his way to my right breast, circling my nipple with his tongue before pulling it into his mouth before doing the same on the other side. He tweaked one nipple with the tips of his fingers and sucked on the other. I bucked beneath him, groaning his name, pleading. He took pity on me by pulling back and continuing his slow torture down the center of my stomach, licking, nipping, placing wet kisses on me. When he finally reached my mound, he stopped and looked up. Our gazes met and held.

"I'm not sure I can take it," I whispered.

"I'm not sure I can either." His tongue swiped over my clit. My eyes shut as my entire body shook. "Eyes on me, Sprite."

I gave him what he wanted and my heart beat out of my chest as he lowered his mouth onto me again, giving another long lick. He groaned against me.

"I missed this so fucking much," he said.

Those were the last words he spoke before his mouth really started moving against me, licking, sucking my clit into his mouth, making sounds of pleasure that rivaled the ones coming out of my mouth. My hands sank into his hair, pulling as he feasted on me.

When he'd said he was a starving man, I hadn't taken his word at face value, but feeling him and hearing the sounds he was making while I unraveled made me believe him. With one last swipe over my clit, I came undone, pulsing and shouting his name over and over. He nipped at the insides of my thighs as I continued to shake in the aftermath of the orgasm and then made his way back up completely. I'd let go of his hair at some point and was holding on to his muscular shoulders, gripping them as he moved over me. His mouth came back to my neck, sucking there as I dragged my hands down his torso, pressing into each etched muscle, until I reached his board shorts. I pulled them off and he kicked them aside quickly, coming right back to me like he couldn't bear being away from my skin for too long. Our eyes met again.

"I'm clean," he said. "But I'll get a condom, considering . . ." He chuckled mildly.

"I have an IUD, because . . . you know."

A devious smile spread across his lips as he spread my legs farther apart and settled between them, keeping his eyes locked on mine as he pressed the tip of his cock against me. I held my breath, spread my legs farther, tried to stop psyching myself out. I couldn't seem to relax. Rowan noticed and reached to push my still-damp hair out of my face.

"I love you, Sprite," he said, pressing his forehead against mine as he pushed inside me. My breath hitched as he fully entered me. I arched my back. My hands gripped his biceps. "I should've told you years ago." He pulled out excruciatingly slowly. I whimpered. He thrust back in fast. Hard. I gasped, arching once more, my nails digging into his biceps. "I'm sorry I didn't." He pulled out again. Slowly.

"Fuck," I cried. "Stop pulling out like that."

He pushed back in. Hard. Fast. Tears sprung up in my eyes. He brought his mouth to my cheek, my neck, my forehead, breathing out. "Fuck. I missed you so damn much."

He pulled out again. Slowly. The emotion built inside my chest, closing and gripping and pulsating the way my core was. Rowan pushed back in, letting me feel his length, making me squeeze around his girth. He groaned deeply, breathing choppily. He began to thrust without pausing, faster, deeper, pulling me closer and tucking his large hands underneath me to lift me, squeezing my ass with each thrust. He let go of one side and brought a hand between us, circling my clit with his thumb as he continued to thrust. I felt my eyes roll back as he continued the sweet torture. The build got stronger, squeezing my core so tight I was sure I'd explode.

"Look at me, Sprite."

I did and then I started to convulse around him. He thrust a few more times before he followed, grunting out my name.

CHAPTER TWENTY-FIVE

ROWAN

I RAN my fingers through her hair slowly, not wanting to wake her. We hadn't gotten much sleep at all and I didn't want her to blame me if she woke up with dark circles under her eyes. I'd told her I loved her. The thought made my hand pause on her head. I'd told her I loved her and she hadn't said it back. I didn't need her to. I felt it the way I felt my own love for her burning every night through the years. My phone vibrated on the nightstand. I turned over, got out of bed, and picked it up on my way out of the door, shutting it behind me softly.

"Sam, I swear if this is about—"

"Where's Tessa?"

I frowned. "Celia? Why are you calling me from Sam's phone?"

"Where is my sister? I don't have time for this."

"Sleeping. Why? Did something happen? Where's Miles?"

"Miles is fine," she said. I exhaled, but then she continued, "Freddie was in an accident."

"What kind of accident?" My chest tightened. I didn't know much, but I knew Freddie's job was dangerous as hell.

"He got . . . he was in an ambush. I don't know." She choked out her words. "I don't . . . where's Tessa?"

"Where is he? Is he okay?"

"He's in the hospital. They're operating on him now."

"Is he going to be okay?"

"I don't know!" Celia yelled. "I don't know! I need to talk to my sister."

"Is everything okay?" Tessa asked from the doorway to the room. I hadn't even heard it open. I swallowed as our eyes met. I'd never seen someone move as fast as she did. One second, she was in the doorway and the next second, she had grabbed the phone from me and was shouting into it.

"What happened? Is Miles okay?" She let out a breath a second before all the blood drained from her face and I had to steady her shoulders to keep her from falling over.

"But is he okay?" She pressed her hand to her chest. "Celia. How bad is it? Did you see him? Did you see him?" She screamed the last question, her voice grating. "I'll be there as soon as I can."

She handed the phone back to me, turned around, and walked back into the bedroom. I stood there for a second, looked at my phone, and then back toward the bedroom. I dialed Sam's phone back. He answered on the first ring.

"I'm at the hospital," he said. "I came to pick up Miles and take him with me. Everyone is . . . this isn't a good environment for him right now."

"Thank you," I managed to whisper. "Are you taking him to your place?"

"I think it's best. Celia gave me her keys, but I think I'll keep him entertained at the park and my place for now." He exhaled into the phone. "It isn't looking good."

The words hit me in the center of my chest. "What happened?"

"I guess he went into one of his missions and he was ambushed. That's the only thing we know. Are you canceling your meeting?"

"Of course, I'm canceling," I said. The meeting hadn't entered my mind at all. "We'll have to go with what we've got."

"Call me when you land and don't rush. Chloe and I can watch Miles so you don't have to leave Tessa alone."

"Thank you," I said, my throat closed again as I thought about Freddie and what Celia and Tessa must be feeling. I remembered getting the news of my brother's cancer and how my world seemed to shift on an axis. The thought of losing him had my gut twisting every day that first year. I thought of Freddie, who had been like a brother to me growing up, and that same feeling came rushing back. I closed my eyes as I gripped my phone, my brother silent on the other end. "Hey, Sam?"

"Yeah," he whispered.

"I love you." I hadn't said those words to him when he was battling cancer, but I'd felt them, and I was done not saying them.

He was quiet for a couple of beats. "Love you too, Ro."

I hung up and tossed my phone aside to go find Tessa. She wasn't in the room and I could hear the shower on, but when I walked in, I couldn't see the top of her head through the top partition. I walked over and peeked my head in, my chest squeezing when I found her sitting on the floor hugging her legs to her chest. I walked into the shower and sat in front of her, pulling her until she was sitting between my legs. I wrapped my arms around her and stroked her hair as the water hit us.

"He's going to be okay," I whispered, the words burning in my throat. "He's going to be okay."

He had to be okay. She started shaking against me as sobs poured out of her and I held her tighter and whispered the words over and over, willing the universe to listen to me. I'd done it when Sam was sick, and he'd been okay. Maybe it would be the same for Freddie. It had to be.

"Sam has Miles," I said. "He's going to watch him until we get there. We'll go to the hospital and I'll stay as long as you want me to."

I wasn't sure she'd want me to at all. I didn't know what would happen once we got back home. Last night had been amazing, but we still had a long way to go. Loving someone didn't mean everything would automatically work out. We both knew that. I held her until long after the water ran cold and her crying finally subsided. I kissed her forehead as I carefully stood, carrying the weight of her against me and shutting the water off. I let her go to reach for a towel and brought it around her, lifting her hair off her back to dry it separately.

"I n-n-need to get the conditioner off," she said.

I took the towels back, switched the hot water on by itself and pulled her back beneath the spray, turning her to face the wall as I finished washing her hair.

"You washed your body?"

She nodded, turning to face me. She was eye level to my clavicle and in her despondency, that was where she was looking.

"Do you think you can dry yourself while I shower? I'll be two seconds."

"Can I sit there?" She pointed to the little bench behind us. I cupped her face and made her look at me.

"Sweetheart, I need you to do whatever makes you comfortable right now." I ducked down and placed my forehead against hers. She closed her eyes and let out a shaky breath before letting me go and sitting on the bench. As I showered, I watched her dry herself and wrap the towel around her body.

"I hate that stupid company," she said. "The Company, that's what he calls where he works. I hate them. I hate that they call him in the middle of the night and have him doing shit he can't talk about, and I hate the haunted look on his face he comes back with." She wiped her face. I switched off the water and grabbed a towel. "I just want my brother to be okay," she cried. "I don't know life without him."

I wished so badly that I could take the pain away from her, because I would if I could. On our way to the airport, I held her hand. I fought the bricks that threatened to stack back in place around my heart. I fought the old, stupid notion that echoed inside my head, telling me to protect myself, that I didn't bleed. All my life I fought the notion of love because of the effect my parent's marriage had on me. It wasn't until this moment that I realized that even though romantic love was always what I'd shooed away, it wasn't the only thing that scared me. The idea of losing my brother when I thought it might be a possibility was crushing, but the idea of losing Freddie, who was also like a brother to me, was equally as painful. The entire airplane ride back to New York, I held Tessa in my arms, closed my eyes, and hoped for the best.

CHAPTER TWENTY-SIX

TESSA

I COULDN'T TELL you how I arrived in New York. I couldn't tell you how many people were on my flight or what seat I sat in. I couldn't tell you anything before the cab ride over to the hospital because I was in a state of complete shock. I'd somehow managed to speak to Miles and hearing the happiness in his little voice soothed me some. He had been with Samson at the park and then they were going to go to a museum. Miles loved museums. Not for the first time, I was thankful to have someone like Sam in my corner. Rowan reached over and put my hand in his, reminding me that he was also still there.

The cab pulled up in front of the hospital and I didn't wait until it came to a full stop before jumping out and rushing up the sidewalk. I heard Rowan's voice calling out to me, but I only had one thing on my mind: get to Freddie.

I rushed to the security, fished out my license, and paused, looking behind me. Rowan walked inside, dragging both our suitcases behind him, and strode over. He set them down, pulled out his license, and got his visitors' sticker. I followed up with Celia again. Freddie was in the ICU, which meant he out of surgery and alive, which was a relief even though the ICU didn't bring warm and fuzzies with it. Rowan appeared again, taking my hand in his and escorting me toward the elevators. I tightened my grip on his hand as we neared the waiting area for the ICU and let go completely when Celia and I locked eyes. She stood, her eyes bloodshot and puffy, and started to cry the moment she saw me. I felt the emotion surge back as I rushed over to her and wrapped my arms around her.

"What are they saying?"

"He'll live," she said, letting go.

"He's being prepped for another surgery," Dad added. I hadn't even seen him standing there. I threw my arms around him next, crying into his neck the way I had done when I was a kid. When I let go, I hugged Mom and then Grandma Joan.

"Miles is with Sam," my grandmother said.

"I know." I wiped my face.

Rowan was at my side, saying hi to everyone and asking about Freddie. I could feel the tension radiating from him as we sat beside each other. Mom and Dad sat across from us, Celia sat beside me on the other side, and my grandmother beside her.

"I can pick up Miles if you want," Rowan said.

"Would you take him home?"

He brought his hand up and brushed my hair behind my ear. "I'll take him wherever you want him, baby."

"Home," I whispered as I fought back fresh tears.

He pulled my head on top of his shoulder and held me there for a couple of beats.

"What is the company saying?" Celia asked. "Have they said what happened? What he was doing?"

"A mission," Dad said, shrugging. He dragged his hands roughly over his face a couple of times. "They won't say much of anything. They want us to sign papers, but I can't even think right now, let alone sign anything."

"Freddie wouldn't want you to sign anything without his permission," Celia said.

"She's right," I added.

"Well, he's unconscious. The doctors say—" He choked on his words and put his face in his hands, unable to get the sentence out. Mom stood and went over to him, hugging him while he cried. I couldn't stand any of it, but I tried to hold it together.

"Where did he get shot? How?" I asked, raising my voice with each question. "Where the hell was his team? Who did this? We're not signing any papers. They need to give us answers!"

Rowan's thumb moved over my thigh in a soothing manner as I spoke. Dad tracked the movement. He didn't say anything about it, but I knew I'd have to answer questions later.

"His team made it out," Dad said. "I only know this because a guy came by to check on him. Freddie and one of the others were badly hurt."

"And this mission was here in New York?" It must have been for them to bring him to this hospital.

"That was all the information they'd give me."

"This is bullshit." I stood, anger and frustration and blinding fear threatening to overflow inside me, as I paced the short distance to the opposite wall and back. "They need to give us more information. Where was he shot?"

"Spine."

"A spinal injury?" I stopped walking and held on to the back of the nearest chair. "Will he . . . will he walk? Talk?"

"We don't know."

My knees buckled and Rowan was right there to catch me, to keep me upright.

"Come sit down."

I shook my head. I didn't want to sit. I wanted to stand. I wanted my brother to be okay. I wanted him to walk out of that goddamn room and tell me I was stupid for worrying about him. I wanted him to complain about building the IKEA furniture I bought. I wanted him to argue with me over stupid things and tell me I was wrong about everything that came out of my mouth. What would he do if he lost the ability to walk? My brother, who ran everywhere and trained for triathlons for kicks, would hate being restricted. My knees shook again. Rowan's hands tightened.

"Please sit down."

I nodded and let him lead me back to our seats. They weren't paying attention to the way he didn't stop touching me or the way he caressed my hair and whispered that everything would be okay. They didn't notice that he kept touching my face, or my leg, or holding my hands. But I did. I cataloged every movement and the way all of it soothed me and made me feel like I could handle this situation.

CHAPTER TWENTY-SEVEN

ROWAN

AFTER I MADE sure Tessa and her family had eaten, I left the hospital. By the time I got to Sam's apartment, the sun was almost coming up. Thankfully, he let me inside, where I crashed on the couch without another word. It wasn't until I felt someone slapping my face repeatedly that I woke up again, groaning.

"What?"

A little laugh responded. My eyes popped open and landed on Miles's smiling face inches away from mine.

"Hey, Buddy." I smiled, pulling him into a hug. "Don't you know you can't wake people up by hitting them?"

"I tried poking, but Uncle Sam said to slap you."

"Uncle Sam, huh?" I rubbed my eyes and sat up before stretching. "You need a new sofa."

"It's a sofa bed, you know?"

No, I hadn't. It wouldn't have mattered if it had been a rock. I'd been so exhausted when I got here that I hadn't really cared where I'd crashed. I looked at Miles. "What are we doing today?"

"Can we go to the museum?"

"Didn't Uncle Sam take you there yesterday?" I stood, ruffled Miles's hair, and walked to the bathroom, taking the bag I'd packed for Miami with me.

"He wants to go to the one in the city. I took him to the one nearby."

"Hm." I spit out toothpaste and rinsed my mouth. "How's the weather? What about the park? We can go out on the canoe or visit the library. Have you been there yet?"

Miles ran into the bathroom, shaking his head. "Do we have to be quiet there?"

"At the library? Yes." I chuckled. "Is that going to be a problem?"

He shrugged nonchalantly, made a funny face, and walked out. If I hadn't known he was my son, that right there would have given it away. After I finished, I joined my brother in the kitchen.

"How did you not know? He looks just like me." I looked over at Miles, who was busy with a puzzle. If it was one of Sam's puzzles, it would take him all day. Sam liked to do puzzles and crosswords nowadays to help with his memory.

"I told you I suspected. He was a baby. He looked like everyone."

He didn't look like everyone. He looked like *me*. Big difference. I didn't push the matter because at the end of the day, it didn't make a difference.

"How's Freddie?"

I closed my eyes. "I'm torn between going down there and calling. I just don't want to leave Miles again."

"You can leave him with me. We can go get bagels down the block, you can take them while Miles and I eat, and then you can pick him up and go to the library."

"That doesn't sound half bad." I closed my eyes again. "I'm going to need two pounds of coffee to get through this day."

"On it. Go shower."

"On it."

AN HOUR LATER, we were at a bagel shop close to the hospital, standing in the longest line for bagels I'd ever seen.

"They better taste like heaven."

"They do. Check the Yelp reviews if you don't believe me."

"What does heaven taste like?" Miles inquired.

"Good question," I said. "I have no idea."

"Hm." He pursed his lips as he looked around. "So why do you say that?"

I felt myself smile. He was so damn cute. "It's just an expression."

"Like 'bite the bullet'?"

"Yeah, like that," I said, shooting my brother a-what-the-fuck look. "Where did you hear that one?"

"Uncle Freddie says it a lot." His voice was quieter when he said Freddie's name. He blinked up at me. "Is he going to be okay?"

If I'd ever had a doubt about whether hearts could break, seeing the uncertainty in his eyes and not being able to reassure him would have proven to me that it was very possible. I swallowed and nodded as I lifted him into my arms. He wrapped his arms around my neck and settled his head on my chest as if he'd known me his entire life. I held him tighter.

"Uncle Freddie's a strong guy. A soldier, the most badass motherfucker I know," I said. "He's going to be just fine."

I believed the words I spoke because I knew Freddie and if there was ever anyone who could get out of something this serious, it was him. We were finally seated. I carried Miles over to the table, ordered a quick box to go, grabbed one of those bagels, and promised I'd be right back. It took me ten minutes to get to the hospital in an Uber, and when I reached the ICU waiting area, they were all strewn across the chairs. Tessa's parents had their heads leaning on each other's and were asleep. Tessa was lying on two chairs, as was Celia. Joan was the only one up and about, stretching her arms over her head and cracking her neck. She glanced up when she saw me approach with the bagels and coffee.

"You are a savior," she said. "I'm never saying that again, so revel in it."

"How's Freddie?"

"Awake. Finally. The doctor just came by, but I'm letting them sleep a little longer. They're still running tests."

"Any news on the spinal injury thing?"

"Not yet." She took the box of bagels and set it on a side table. I followed her and set down the box of coffee and the cups, then walked over to Tessa. I crouched in front of her and brushed her hair back, needing to touch her.

"You better take care of that girl this time around."

"With my life," I said, standing and facing Joan. "I mean that."

"And Miles."

"Especially Miles."

She narrowed her eyes on me, judging . . . considering, and

then she smiled. "I believe you. How's the divorce coming along?"

"Not fast enough." I ran a hand through my hair. "I don't know what else to do to speed it up."

"Want my advice? Give her what she wants and get yourself a restraining order. Tessa was talking to Celia about it last night and she means it when she says she doesn't want Miles anywhere around that woman." She shrugged, turning back to the bagels. "Don't say I never did you any favors."

A restraining order against Camryn? That seemed extreme. I'd get one if Tessa asked me to but getting one without any other justification than my disdain for the woman didn't feel right. I said goodbye to Joan and let her know where I was taking Miles for the day. On my way back to the bagel shop, I mulled over what she'd said. I'd known Camryn my entire life. I knew she wasn't capable of physically harming anyone. Would she? I shook the thought away. No. She wouldn't. She was too self-involved for that.

When I got back there, Miles was finishing up his eggs and bacon. I told him and Sam the good news about Freddie being awake.

"What happened with the fabrics lady?" Sam asked as I sipped on my coffee.

"I called her before we left Miami, she understood our situation and is willing to Skype with Tessa about the fabrics. We'll see what happens."

MILES THOUGHT the library was cool, but too quiet, so we didn't stay long before moving on to the Children's Museum. There, he ran around and played registrar while I shopped for pretend-groceries.

"Bread goes in a baggie," he said, pointing at me. "Remember that next time, mister."

I chuckled. This kid was something else. He had a response for every item I put on the tiny conveyer belt.

"What about oranges?" I asked. "They have a shell. Do they need a baggie?"

This gave Miles pause. "But if you have more than one orange, you'll drop them everywhere."

"That is true." I chuckled. "Baggies it is."

We moved on to the fishing exhibition, where you grab plastic fishing rods and toss them into a pond they had in hopes of catching magnetic fish. Miles's eyes lit up every time he got a bite.

"You're good at this. Have you ever been fishing?"

"No."

"Not even at Joan's?"

"Nana's gonna take me soon."

"I'll take you," I said. "If your mom agrees."

"Okay." He smiled wide. "Can mommy come?"

"Of course."

"Can Uncle Sam and Chloe come?"

"Of course."

"Can Cody come?"

My eyes snapped to his. I wanted to say fuck no but thought better of it. Instead, I gave a small nod. "Sure."

I needed to talk to Tessa about that, but now wasn't the time. We finished up in the museum and walked out and down the street. My stomach growled when I saw the Indian place down the block, but something told me that Miles wouldn't be too thrilled with eating there. We ended up at a pizza joint that sold pizza by the slice. This, he liked. It was either the best pizza I'd ever eaten or I was just starving.

Tessa had sent a few texts throughout the day asking if everything was okay and keeping me posted on what she knew about

Freddie, but by the time we got to their apartment, we hadn't texted in at least an hour, which made me think that she was starting to trust me with him. Upstairs, I put away the leftover pizza and went into his room to take out his pajamas and get him ready for bed.

"Does mommy give you a bath or do you bathe yourself?" I asked.

"Mommy does."

"Okay. Let's do that first then."

I filled the tub and poured some of the bubble bath he said Tessa used for him. I watched as he played with what he said were PJ Masks toys and joined him even though according to him I did every single voice wrong. He followed that up by telling me that his mommy always did the voices the right way, which seemed to be the running theme for the day. I wanted to point out that he used the same exact voice for each character, but I wasn't three and I didn't take offense to his observation.

It took a couple of minutes longer than I anticipated to get him out of the tub because he wanted to keep playing. In the end, I bribed him with popcorn and a movie.

Once he was dressed in his pajamas, I put on his movie of choice, which was *Frozen*. I'd heard a few Dads talk about it during galas and networkers. They hated it, but it was a pretty cool movie. I'd have to ask Tessa what her thoughts on it were. Miles fell asleep before the girl with the brown hair got to the trolls, which was a shame since that song was the best one I'd heard thus far. I picked up his little body and took him to his bed, mimicking everything I'd seen Tessa do the other night.

I switched off the television in the living room and went to Tessa's bedroom, turning the movie back on there instead, not because I liked it but because I couldn't start watching a movie and not finish it.

CHAPTER TWENTY-EIGHT

TESSA

MY APARTMENT WAS quiet when I walked in the door. I wasn't sure what I'd expected. It was past Miles's curfew, after all. I guess deep down, I wasn't sure that Rowan could actually handle it all, but everything was spotless and Miles was sleeping soundly in his bed. I walked quietly to the bathroom and looked in there. I could smell the bubble bath I limited to Saturdays only since Miles had a hard time getting out of the tub when I let him use it. I smiled, imagining the way he'd probably given Rowan the runaround and convinced him to let him do the bubbles. When I walked into my room, the television and the lights were off, but he'd left the bathroom light on, and I could make out his sleeping form. I showered quickly and dressed in a long T-shirt and boy shorts before joining him in bed. He stirred when I kissed him.

"Hm." He wrapped an arm around me, pulling me flush against him. "Missed you."

The words curled inside me. Was this how it would always be between us? "Missed you too. Thanks for breakfast and for taking care of Miles."

His eyes opened slowly. "Don't thank me for any of that."

"Not a lot of people would have done either of those things."

"I'm not a lot of people. Miles is my son and you, Tessa Monte, are my world. I'd do anything for either of you."

His words spread warmth inside me. I snuggled into him. "Did he con you into the bubble bath?"

"Not much of a con when all he does is mention mommy. 'Mommy lets me. Mommy does this. Mommy, Mommy, Mommy.' I wasn't sure if I wanted to slap you or make love to you when you got here."

I smiled against the crook of his neck. "What's the status on that?"

"I'm not sure yet." He yawned. "How's Freddie?"

"Alive." My voice shook as I said the words. "The doctors say he'll be fine and able to walk. I wasn't able to see him though. It'll have to be tomorrow. I was too tired to wait."

"I bet." He kissed my shoulder, my neck. My pulse quickened. "Go to sleep."

But I didn't want to go to sleep. My emotions were running rampant and I wasn't sure if I could attempt turning them off. I wanted to talk about things, but more than anything, I wanted to feel him inside me again. I wanted him to give me one of those searing kisses that made me forget what day of the week it was. I said this aloud and he responded with a little growling sound that seemed to come from the back of his throat.

"You need rest, baby."

"I need you more."

He scooted close and pressed his lips against mine, his tongue coaxing my mouth open. He kissed me with the fervor of a starving man, as if he hadn't taken his fill the other night, and I matched it because it was how he made me feel—utterly needy for him. He positioned us so that I was on top of him, straddling the length of him. I took advantage, even with both of us still dressed, grinding down on him and reveling in the feeling of him pressing against me, of my lips on his.

"Rowan," I moaned to let him know I needed more. He wrapped his hand around the back of my neck and sat up as I moved, his hips lifting to the rhythm of mine, meeting me where I needed him. "I'm going to—"

"I know, baby."

And then I was shaking with the orgasm. He used the moment to sit up against the headboard, yanking his T-shirt off and tossing it aside. His hands came back to my sides and he did the same to me, peeling off my T-shirt and tossing it aside, his fingers hooking into my shorts and underwear, making me shimmy out of them and come right back to him, the only fabric separating us was that of his boxer briefs, which I pulled down before he rolled so I was tucked beneath him.

He was fully covering my body, his mouth coming down on every inch of me—my neck, my chest, tugging each nipple into his mouth softly, then biting as he let go. I shook beneath him from that alone. He did it again and again until I was panting audibly. Then he made his way down my stomach, which quivered with the feel of his beard grating against it. I grabbed his hair on instinct. His gaze snapped to mine, those blue eyes darkening into a pool of desire that I'd gladly drown in.

"Ro," I heard myself whisper, my voice hoarse. He pressed his mouth to my mound, a soft kiss. I shifted, my body contorting this way and that to get his mouth where I needed it. I gripped his hair tighter. "Rowan."

"Yeah?"

"Please do something."

"I am doing something." The corners of his mouth lifted slightly.

"I feel like I'm going to explode."

"That's the point, babe."

"Rowan," I grated, drawing out the word as he licked between my folds once, twice. I wouldn't be able to handle this. I'd die. I knew I would. I gripped his hair harder. He chuckled.

"If you wanted me to shave my head, you could've told me."

"Not funny." I moved against him.

"That's right, baby," he said, his voice hoarse. "Grind on my face."

I did just that, moving against his tongue, his fingers, which joined and plunged into me as he licked my clit. The build came on fast, the pressure mounting in my core with each dirty word he spoke. I squeezed my eyes shut, throwing my head back, my body thrashing as he continued to pump his fingers inside me, his tongue lavishing me, his deep groan welcoming the orgasm he pulled out of me.

His mouth made its way back up my body. I thought he'd pause to kiss me, hold me. I had it on the tip of my tongue to ask for more when he spread my legs farther apart and thrust inside me, burying himself to the hilt, making me feel like I couldn't move an inch. I felt. Him everywhere. I cried out again, digging my nails into his biceps.

"Rowan."

His gaze held mine as he thrust in and out, in an unrushed state, taking his time with each stroke, letting me feel him completely. I sucked in a shaky breath. It all felt like too much. I'd wanted to. Let go of everything building inside me, but the way he was looking at me only added more weight, making me feel fuller.

"I love you," he said again and again, as if he needed to make sure the words would sink in. He tweaked my nipples with his fingers, slowing his pace, pulling in and out slowly as he brought his face to the crook of my neck. "Don't ever leave me, baby."

And that plea spilling from his lips was what did it for me. I tightened around him as he groaned my name, and as I climaxed again, I brought a hand up to his face, held his gaze and said, "I love you, Rowan Hawthorne."

CHAPTER TWENTY-NINE

TESSA

I SAT behind my desk and dialed Natasha's number on the Skype of my computer, gearing myself up for an argument, but the woman who answered the video call was not only soft-spoken and incredibly polite but also absolutely stunning, with dark hair and pale skin. She looked like Snow White.

"Natasha?" I asked to be sure.

"Yes." She smiled. "You're Tessa."

Her English was great too. "I'm so sorry we couldn't make our meeting the other—"

"Oh, my goodness please." She waved a hand, securing a

flyaway hair into her sleek ponytail. "How's your brother? Is everything okay?"

"He's still in the hospital, but the outlook is good."

"If you don't mind my asking, what happened?"

"He . . . his job is dangerous and puts him in the line of fire sometimes. Quite literally." I wasn't sure how much information I could divulge about it, not that I knew enough to be harmful, but still.

"I'm so sorry," she offered, and she actually looked sorry. "I hope he'll be okay."

"He will be. He's a strong boy." I smiled a little, taking a breath. "So, the fabric?"

"Yes. The fabric." She brightened up and pulled a large swatch of royal blue leather into the camera's view. "Mr. Hawthorne said you were looking for something like this."

My heart pounded against my chest as I looked at the fabric. I didn't want to jump the gun and shout that it was exactly what I was looking for, but it really was, and I was awful at hiding my emotions. "That's exactly what I need."

"He said you need the leather for a car? And then more bohemian fabrics for a boutique hotel?"

"Yes." I didn't bother to rein in my excitement, my eyes still on the fabric in her hands. "Where did you get that?"

"Colombia." She said it with pride—or, as my grandmother would say, with gusto.

"And you won't sell it to a man," I said, which had her cheeks flushing prettily as she shook her head.

"It isn't that I'm a man-hater. I'm sure that's what it seems like to everyone. I know no one is interested in my life story or anything, so I won't bore you with it, but I had a lot of harm done to me and my company by men who profited while the rest of us scraped by. I refuse to let that continue."

"I think it's commendable."

"Thank you."

"I'd also love to buy your fabrics. You'd make good money," I offered. "Our acquisitions person is a man, though, so you'd have to deal with him."

"But the project is yours."

"The projects are mine." I smiled brightly, the way I did every time I thought about the position I was in. "And as long as I can get these done in time and do them right, I'll have more projects and need more fabrics."

"Okay. I'm sold."

"You are?" I think I squealed it. She laughed.

"I am."

We decided that she'd overnight me the fabrics the minute I transferred the money into her account and she'd fly up next week to meet with Ryan Ford and sign contracts. When it was settled, I informed the team and headed to the hospital.

When I got there, Celia was walking out of Freddie's room with one hand on her stomach and another over her mouth, visibly upset. I rushed over to her, catching her as she nearly fell over.

"What happened? What happened? Is he okay?" I looked up at the closed door.

She nodded, still crying, unable to get a word out. I let go of her and ran into the room, stopping at the foot of the bed when I saw the doctor, two nurses, and my parents who were around his bed. What held me in place was the sight of my brother, my big brother, lying in the middle of a hospital bed with bandages on his head and face. Had he been shot in the face? Something wasn't adding up. They'd said his spine, and what I saw was a mummy-looking thing that they said was my brother.

"Maybe you should wait with your sister," Dad said, his arm around my mom's shoulders.

"What's going on?" I walked closer, my fingers running over

the edge of the bed, keeping my eyes on his wrapped head. Freddie's right arm moved, his fingers twitching. I grabbed them and curled my own around them. The only thing I could make out was his brown eyes and lips, which seemed to have a gash running through the left side.

"They just re-bandaged me. You missed the unveiling," he said, his voice hoarse. The emotion I'd been holding back bubbled in my throat and finally erupted along with the tears I'd been holding back.

"I didn't think you were going to make it."

"You thought I was going to miss your birthday?"

"You could've died," I whispered. "For years, I had gone to sleep praying that you'd make it back home from your deployments, and then this happens in our own soil? It isn't okay, Freddie."

"I was working." He squeezed my hand harder.

"You need to quit. We can't lose you. I can't lose you. *Miles* can't lose you." The lump in my throat got bigger. I used my free hand to wipe my face. "Please don't go back there."

He didn't respond, but his hand shook in mine, and I took that as confirmation that he wouldn't.

"Will you . . . how's your spine?"

"I'll be walking in no time," he said, "Look at my foot. I can wiggle my toes and everything."

"Stop it, Freddie." I swallowed thickly, unable to find humor in his words. I eyed the bandages. "What happened to your face?"

"Just a little scratch."

Mom let out a loud sob behind me and I knew little was probably not the word for it. Selfishly, I didn't care because the fact remained that my brother was alive.

I GOT HOME AT FIVE, just as Ray, the tutor, was leaving the apartment, and he caught me up on what he had just been working on with Miles. Then I set my things down and walked into the kitchen. Miles spotted me first, smiling wide and running over to me with open arms.

"I missed you so much," I said into his hair. "How was tutoring?"

"Good, and Ray brought me this." He held up a little square with colorful shapes. "It's called a Tangram."

"That looks very cool." I kissed him on the cheek and turned to Rowan, who was wearing my Minnie Mouse apron. He hadn't tied it behind his back, probably because it was too small. I laughed as I walked over to him.

"You look cute."

He shot me a look. "I have a meeting with my lawyer in a couple of hours and I didn't want to get dirty."

He reached down and kissed me softly. I looked in Miles's direction on instinct and sure enough, he was looking right at us. To my surprise, he was smiling. He went back to the little colorful square thing.

"What kind of meeting?"

"Divorce stuff," he said and then grinned wide. "But Sam and I are officially the owners of Hawthorne Industries."

"Oh my god!" I threw my arms around him. "That's so awesome. Why are you not excited?"

"I am." He exhaled. "I didn't exactly want this to go through before the divorce, but I'll live. My lawyer found some loopholes in case Camryn starts harassing me for the company."

"Oh. I didn't even think of that."

"But hey, I own the company. I'm happy about that." He smiled.

"Me too." I smiled.

The divorce needed to be out of the way and everything

would be settled. My stomach clenched at the mere thought of how long it could take. If Camryn wanted to be a real bitch, she'd drag it out. For all of our sakes, I hoped she was seeing her Wall Street guy and envisioning a future with him. Just thinking about that made me angry. Here she was making Rowan jump through hoops to get out of the agreement when all the while she was shacking up with another man. An uneasy feeling settled in the pit of my stomach. I told Miles to go and play while Rowan and I finished making dinner. Not that I was doing anything, but Miles didn't point that out.

"Did you ever give Camryn an indication that you may be in love with her?" It pained me to get the words out. Rowan's brows pulled in.

"Never."

"You never—" I swallowed, clearing my throat. "Slept with her?"

He put the spatula down and turned to me, his handsome face crumbling a bit. That was the only answer I needed. I was almost glad he was wearing that ridiculous Minnie Mouse apron.

"Tessa, it was only—"

I put a hand up. "I'm sorry I asked."

"It happened once. I was drunk and—"

I shut my eyes. "You were married for nearly four years. I didn't exactly expect you to become a monk or stay faithful to the idea that maybe, possibly, we'd—"

"But I did." He stepped closer, his hand coming up to tilt my chin. "It was a stupid, one-time mistake, and I can't take it back, but I swear I never led her on. I never led her to believe we'd ever become anything real. I was waiting for you. I was planning for you."

"To be honest, I don't think I would care if you'd slept with other women. It's the Camryn thing that gets me," I said quietly.

"The thought of her getting you all those years . . . I hate it. I can barely stand to think about it."

Rowan brought his lips down to mine softly, his thumb brushing my jaw as he held my face. "I understand," he said. "I feel the same way about you and other men, but I'm yours. I have always been yours. I will forever be yours."

His words lifted the weight from my chest. I walked over to the table and started setting it while he finished plating the food.

"We need to talk about a few more things," he said, coming over and setting Miles's *Lion Guard* plate and a salad on the table first.

"What?" I went back and served us glasses of water.

"You have my son taking Singapore math tutoring for kicks?" He glanced at me as we walked by each other, heading in opposite directions.

"He likes it."

"He isn't even four."

"He'll be four soon enough."

"Tessa." He stopped and stared at me. "Singapore math? I had to google it to see what the hell it was when the tutor got here."

"My roommate in college took Singapore math since age three, and she was a genius. Like, a real genius. She's probably discovering the cure for cancer as we speak."

"You know who else was also a genius? Bill Gates. Do you think he took Singapore math?"

I shrugged. "I haven't read his autobiography."

"Tessa."

I crossed my arms. "I'm not taking him out of tutoring because you feel like he needs to do more boyish things."

"Are you saying this because you don't feel like I can make decisions in our son's life or because you genuinely want him to spend his time doing math?"

I opened my mouth and closed it, frowning. A little bit of both, I realized. He had just waltzed into our lives. For me, it was different because I knew Ro. I'd known him my entire life and had been in love with him most of it as well. Miles just met him. Yes, that was his son, but it didn't change the fact that Rowan was new in his life. He was just a boy.

"Miles," I called out. "Television off. Wash your hands and come sit down, baby."

He groaned but switched the television off and sulked as he walked to the bathroom. I was glad he hadn't chosen this moment to argue about it because I wasn't sure I could handle two Hawthorne boys bickering at once. Rowan walked over to me, blocking my path and placing his hands on either side of my body, effectively caging me in.

"You didn't tell me he was my son." His voice was incredibly low. "You stripped me of the rights a present father has. I understand your reasons. I do. I even partially agree with them, but don't think I won't push until you give me my rightful place in this house."

"I know." I lifted my hand to his face, the scuff on it tickling my palm. "That isn't fair of me and I'm sorry. I'll try to be better about that."

He kissed my palm. "We both have work to do."

"I agree, but the tutor stays." Time seemed to suspend as we looked at each other. I was only aware of the heat of his body against mine and the desire in his eyes as he looked at me. Desire we couldn't act on with Miles about to walk into the room. "Do you miss your house?"

His brows pulled. "What?"

"Do you miss being home?"

"I miss having all of my clothes," he said. "Why?"

"Just wondering if you're ready to go home yet."

His lips twitched. "You think I'm going back there without you?"

"Well—"

"I won't be going home and staying there unless you're willing to pack up and come with me."

"I can't just—"

"Marry me."

My heart stopped beating. "What?"

"Marry me."

"You're already married."

"As soon as I get out of this bind, I want you to marry me."

I laughed, shaking my head. "This is absurd."

"Is it?" He pinned me with a look that made me question my own words. "What's stopping us from being together?"

"Your marriage to Camryn."

"Aside from that, smart ass."

"That's a big factor."

"I'm taking care of that," he murmured, bringing my hand to his mouth and kissing it.

"I don't know," I whispered.

"Do you want to make this work?"

"Yes."

"Okay then. It's settled." His eyes lit up mischievously. I shook my head. "Oh, and Cody needs to go."

"What? Go where? What are you talking about?" I couldn't remember the last time I'd spoken to Cody.

"I was talking to Miles about going to Joan's cottage and he asked me if Cody could come with us. I want him out of the picture."

I pulled back and stared at him. "You're serious."

"As a fucking heart attack."

"Oh my—" I laughed. It felt so good. "Cody isn't a threat to you and you know it."

"Of course, I know it. That doesn't mean I like him around."

"He's in the fashion industry, Ro."

"So am I. You don't see me trying to get in every woman's pants every two seconds."

"Rowan." I rolled my eyes. "I don't think it's necessary, but if it makes you feel better, I'll tell him you and I are together."

"For good." He shot me a pointed look. "Tell him we're getting married."

I bit my lip to keep from laughing, "I'll make sure to send him an invite to the wedding."

"See? Now we're on the same page."

I laughed loudly but sobered up at the serious expression on his face. I still hadn't officially told Miles about Rowan, mainly because I wanted to do it when it was just the two of us. I didn't want Rowan to be around in case Miles said anything that might unintentionally hurt him and I wanted Miles to know that he was still my number one, my baby boy, and no one would ever take his place in my heart. Rowan tilted my chin again. I met his gaze.

"If I wasn't in this sham of a marriage and I asked you, would you say yes?"

"Maybe." My heart swooshed in my ears.

"Would you have said yes four years ago?"

"Absolutely."

"I'm going to make it so that your maybe turns back into an absolutely."

"Okay."

He pulled back and finished bringing our food—spaghetti with meatballs—to the table. It was delicious. We sat at the table and had dinner like a normal family as he asked about Freddie. Of course, I gave him the watered-down version of what had happened in the hospital. I didn't want Miles the worrywart freaking out over his uncle.

"What happened with Natasha?" Rowan asked as we ate.

"Oh my gosh! I got the contract! Well, Ryan needs to finalize the paperwork, but she agreed."

"That's incredible." He smiled wide. "I lost count of how many times I tried to convince her to sell anything to me."

"I guess you aren't as convincing as you think you are."

"I'll show you how convincing I can be." He winked. I felt myself flush.

He looked over at Miles who was watching the two of us closely. "You know, Miles is an excellent registrar."

"Is that so?" I smiled at Miles.

"He even knows what produce items need to be in little baggies before being placed on a conveyer belt." Rowan's eyes shone with pride. I couldn't stop grinning.

"Bananas don't need baggies," Miles said.

"What about grapes?" Rowan asked.

"Grapes come in a baggie, silly." Miles giggled.

"What about apples?"

Miles tilted his head. "Apples . . . don't, but it's messy."

Rowan chuckled. "You don't want to drop your apples everywhere, right?"

"Right."

"What about kiwi?" I asked.

"Baggies," Miles said quickly.

We went on like this for the next thirty minutes, joking about grocery store items, and despite my exhaustion and the worry I was carrying around for Freddie, I felt whole, and as I looked at Rowan, I realized that if he asked me to marry him right then, I'd say yes, no question.

CHAPTER THIRTY

ROWAN

THE MEETING with my lawyer went as well as I'd hoped. Camryn finally filed her response and asked for more money, as I expected. While my lawyer suggested I try to get her to come down and agree on a smaller settlement, I said no. I'd give her whatever she wanted as long as she let me walk away from this. It was that thought that had me walking a little lighter the next morning as I took Miles to daycare. Tessa went to visit Freddie at the hospital before work, but said she'd be home early enough to pick up Miles from school and take him to karate. She didn't want to overwhelm me with things, she'd said, as if my child would ever be a burden to me.

"You know Daeshon with the Spider-Man book bag?" Miles asked as we walked hand in hand.

"I have no clue who Daeshon is."

"He said his mommy and daddy live with him." He glanced up at me, squinting against the sun. My heart thrashed in my chest. "Are you going to live with us forever?"

My heart jumped. Tessa hadn't told him that I was his father yet. I'd been giving her time and with everything going on with Freddie it wasn't really a priority. "Do you want me to live with you forever?"

"Yes." He gave a nod. I loved the way he pronounced his s like sh.

"You really want me to live with you forever?" I stopped walking and lifted him into my arms with a grin. "Do you think your mom will say yes?"

"Yes." He nodded again. "She loves you."

"She loves me? Did she tell you that?"

"No. I can tell."

"How can you tell?"

He shrugged. "I know Mommy."

I chuckled, gave him a kiss on the cheek, and then carried him the rest of the way to school, which was only half a block.

"Behave, learn, and be kind to everyone," I said, setting him back on his feet and straightening his sweater. He smiled wide, giving me a nod.

"What the fuck is this?"

A cold wave of dread trickled down my spine at the sound of Camryn's squeal behind me. On instinct, I grabbed Miles and pulled him into my chest, shielding him. I glanced up.

"What are you doing here?"

"You have a son?" she shouted. "Are you fucking kidding me?"

"Camryn, I'm only going to ask you this one time, please get away from here." I made my voice as calm and clear as possible and then carried Miles against my chest until we reached his teacher. "Please take him inside." I looked at Miles, whose eyes were wide and clearly scared. I kissed his forehead, saying, "Everything is okay, buddy, just go inside with Ms. Porter."

She must have seen how worried I was, because she picked him up into her arms and walked right in.

Camryn continued screaming, "You thought you could hide this? You thought you could keep him from me? Who the hell do you think you are?"

I walked over to her, trying my best to keep my composure. Never in my life would I hit a woman, but with the way the rage building inside me was making me shake, I couldn't be sure. I fished out my phone and called the police to tell them where I was. By the time they got here, they'd either have to take her or me, but one of us would leave in a cop car. I stepped out of the school gates and heard her scream some more. She looked like a lunatic, completely unlike the pacifist, well-composed Camryn I'd always known. I made my way down the street, away from the school, hoping she'd follow. The last thing I needed was to grab her by the arm and have her claim I was mistreating her.

"What is your problem?"

"My problem?" she seethed. "My problem is that I knew something was going on when you agreed to the demands I gave my lawyer, but I didn't expect this. Whose is he?" Her voice rose with each word.

Finally, a patrol car pulled up. I waved the officer down.

"He is a cheating, lying scum!" she screamed as the police officer rushed over to us.

I explained the problem to the police officer, making sure he knew she did this in front of the students and teachers of the school.

"We'll have to file an incident report," he said calmly. Camryn began to cry loudly. The officer's partner, a woman, came over and asked more questions. I answered them all—the child was mine, not hers, I was in the middle of a divorce, etcetera.

"Quite the telenovela you have here," the officer said.

"Did she threaten the child?" the woman asked.

"No." If she had, this probably would have ended far differently from how it was.

"Do you think she'd harm the child?" the second officer asked again, eyeing Camryn, who was now shaking as she sobbed harder.

"I don't think so," I said. I'd known her my entire life. She wasn't capable of physically harming someone, least of all a child.

"You want my advice?" the other officer said, writing something down.

I looked at him and waited.

"File for an order of protection."

"What do I do about her right now?" I glanced at Camryn.

"We'll handle that," the woman officer said.

"Is there any way to keep her away from the school?"

"Get down to the station as soon as you get a chance and file a restraining order."

I stuck around to make sure Camryn didn't lie while recounting what happened. She took the blame. Every time she got to the part where she had to talk about Miles, she broke down again. I didn't have it in me to feel bad for her. I felt bad for my son, who had to witness that before being sent inside his classroom without so much as an explanation. Tessa was going to kill me. This was exactly what she was afraid of. Maybe she was right to keep Miles from me all this time if this was how Camryn was going to act. None of those thoughts helped the dread that sank into the pit of my stomach as I thought about having to tell her what happened.

CHAPTER THIRTY-ONE

TESSA

I GLANCED up from my desk as Chloe knocked and opened the door, Rowan behind her.

"What are you doing here?" I pushed my chair back and stood.

He walked into the office and stopped, taking it all in. I could tell he was impressed by the way his brow arched, but the serious expression on his face made me worry about his reason for being here at all.

"I'll be out there," Chloe said. "Shout if you need me."

"Thanks, Chlo." I looked at Rowan. "What's going on?"

"We need to talk."

"Okay." I sat, not liking the way he said those words. He took a seat across from me, folding his hands on the other side of my desk.

"It's about a couple of things. One is Camryn," he said, closing his eyes. "I fucked up."

My stomach turned. How many times could we go through this? "Fucked up how?"

"She showed up at Miles's school this morning."

"What? Where's Miles?" I stood again.

"He's fine. I went back and checked on him, spoke to him, he's fine."

"Why didn't you call me?"

"I didn't want to tell you this over the phone. I promise, he's okay." I must have looked ready to run out the door because he said, "Tessa, I promise. Nothing is going to happen to him."

I forced myself to remain seated even though it really was the last thing I wanted to do. "What happened?"

He recounted what happened from the way Camryn showed up and caused a scene to the police showing up afterward.

"You filed for an order of protection?"

"I couldn't," he said, swallowing thickly. "I'm not Miles's legal guardian. My name isn't on his birth certificate, so . . . "

He let the words hang. Under any other circumstance, I would have given those words a little more acknowledgment, but as the calm passed and the rage began to slowly creep through me, the only thing I could do was think about killing Camryn. I'd kill her. I'd fucking choke the hell out of her. How dare she show up at my son's daycare? How dare she look at him? How dare she—

"Tess, say something," Rowan whispered across from me.

"I hate her."

"I know and I swear I'd rather die before she did anything

that would hurt Miles in any way. I don't think she would. I don't want her near him, but I don't think she'd do anything to a little boy."

I felt sick, so sick. I slumped in the chair again, putting my elbows on the desk. I buried my face in my hands. "You don't know that."

The next second had him kneeling on the floor next to my chair, his hand on my shoulder. I didn't shove him away, even though a part of me wanted to.

"She doesn't know Miles is yours. I'm afraid if she found out . . ." He let loose a deep breath. "I couldn't bear it, baby."

He couldn't bear it? I nearly laughed at that, but I knew it was unfair. He'd been watching Miles, taking care of him, being a father to him. In truth, I wasn't sure what I would have done without Rowan these last couple of weeks.

But this?

This was major and brought on a wave of fear I'd never felt. Camryn could go after me all she wanted, but my son was off limits, and if she didn't even know he was mine . . . fear gripped my chest. I lowered my hands and looked up at Rowan, who looked completely at a loss for words. He was chewing on his bottom lip as he watched me, waiting for the verdict. He knew it would be bad. It had to be.

"You need to stay away from us until the divorce is final."

His face fell. "What? No. I can't not see you. I can't not see my son."

"Your son is the reason I'm asking you to do this. For him, because of him, you need to stay away until this is all final and we figure out how to make sure she stays away from us."

"Tessa—"

"You can Skype with him, talk on the phone, whatever you want, but please wait until she's out of your life before you come crashing back into ours. He's a baby." The look in his eyes nearly broke me in two, but my son was my priority. "He bleeds, you know. Our little boy bleeds."

"I know he does," he said brokenly. "And out of all the things I'm proud of, that one's at the top of the list." He cupped my face, leaned down, and kissed me softly. "I love you, Sprite. Don't forget that."

CHAPTER THIRTY-TWO

ROWAN

"SO IT GOES," Dean said, taking a swig of the glass bottle of Coke in his hand. "You get the chick, lose the chick, hope to God you can get the chick back again."

"Are you speaking from experience?"

"Fuck no. I don't have time to play those games," he said. "I fuck. I leave. That's it."

"Which is a game in and of itself."

"Yeah, but I'm a pro at that game."

I chuckled, waiting for him to give me whatever information he wanted to tell me. He'd called me and asked me to meet him for it. Dean was odd like that. I got the feeling he thought the CIA was listening in on every phone call he made. Shit, maybe they were.

"Camryn is living with Roger Wales full time." He reached into his jacket and handed me a white envelope. "Pictures in case you need proof in court."

"I'm hoping it doesn't go that far."

"Did you file a restraining order?"

"Tessa filed a complaint on Miles's behalf." I hadn't felt the need to do it for myself and as far as I knew, Tessa hadn't gotten one either. We probably both came to the same conclusion—she was like a gnat, annoying and persistent but harmless.

"Why do you help me?" I asked. It was something that had been grating at me since the first time he showed up after we met at the bar. "You don't let me pay you and you sure as fuck don't seem like the kind of guy who does pro-bono for kicks."

"Pro-bono is one of the ways I repent for past sins."

"Hm. My hopefully soon-to-be brother-in-law has that outlook on life. Too bad his golden heart nearly got him killed."

"How so?"

"He worked for this private company that sent him on some home mission. Totally fucked him up. Got shot up, stabbed, you name it."

"Sounds like it's time to retire."

"I hope so, for everyone's sake. His family hasn't left the hospital much."

"Was he one of the guys in the container raid down by the docks?"

I stopped walking. "How did you know?"

"It was in the paper."

I looked at him for a beat. It had been on the news too, but how did he just put two and two together? I shook the thought away. Dean found out things about everyone around me, he obviously had done the same to Freddie.

"I hope he recovers quickly." He tossed the bottle into the recycling and shook my hand. "Later, kid."

With that, he walked off. I shook my head, took the pictures out of the envelope, and looked through them. I'd definitely give these to my lawyer just in case.

CHAPTER THIRTY-THREE

TESSA

THE DAYS SEEMED to drag on without Rowan in them. I tried not to even look at him while he Skyped with Miles. It made me miss him too much and seeing him only reminded me of how unfair it all was. We spoke on the phone briefly before bed, but it wasn't enough. None of it was. What I didn't do was allow myself to pull back on my feelings. He'd told me he loved me. He'd shown me he loved our son. He just needed to get his shit together and come back to us for good. Those were the thoughts that kept me going as I yanked the door to the hospital open.

When I stepped off the elevator, Celia was standing there with a smile on her face.

"He walked today."

I grinned so wide that my lips cracked from the cold. "How far?"

"Just to the other side of the room," she said. "But he walked."

"How's he handling the scar?"

Her face fell. "Not that great. He keeps making jokes about it, and you know he only makes jokes—"

"When he's depressed. Fuck." I breathed out. "What can we do?"

"Just keep reminding him that the scar doesn't matter. I don't know." She hugged me quickly. "Happy birthday, sissy. I'll see you later."

I walked toward Freddie's room, knocking once before I went inside. I completely froze, my heart galloping in my ears at the sight of Rowan sitting in the chair beside Freddie's bed. It wasn't the first time I'd seen him here. Ever since he figured out what times I visited, he'd come around the same time. Yet, it did nothing to diminish the way I felt each time I saw him.

"Um, hi." I made myself walk inside, letting the door shut behind me. "I didn't bring anything," I said awkwardly.

My brother raised his good eyebrow. "When do you ever bring anything?"

"Shut up, I've been caught up in things."

"I'll forgive you, but only because it's your birthday." He smiled, cringing. I hated seeing him in pain. The scar on the left side of his face curved in the shape of a hook, narrowly missing his eye. It was still bright pink, but the doctors assured everyone that it would fade in time. It wouldn't ever heal completely, but it would get better. I walked over and kissed him on the forehead before going around the bed. Rowan stood before I reached him, wrapping his arms around me and pulling me against him.

"Happy birthday, baby. God, I miss you," he said against my hair. I wrapped my arms around his strong torso and breathed him in, bottling up the scent for later. We let go at the sound of Freddie shifting on the bed.

"I heard you banned him from the apartment," my brother said when Rowan and I pulled away from each other.

"I didn't exactly ban him. Oh, I almost forgot." I reached into my messenger bag and took out the card Miles had made Freddie and another he'd made Rowan. "I didn't know you'd be here, but I've been holding on to this just in case."

His face broke into a grin. "He made one for me?"

I watched both of them as they opened their cards. Freddie's said "Get Well Soon" and had rockets and paint brushes and easels drawn all over it. Rowan's said "I Miss You" and had rockets and pancakes and bacon and books. His smile faltered as he looked at the card, his thumb brushing over it slowly. He looked up after a couple of beats.

"Thank you."

I nodded once, not knowing how to handle the emotion Rowan was showing me. "I have to go. I just wanted to come by before my day gets crazy. I have to go to the hotel to measure the spaces for the furniture."

"Are you getting me a free room?" Freddie asked. "Maybe they can hook it up with a permanent room for me there."

"You have an apartment. Why would you want a hotel room?" I asked. He raised his good eyebrow. I rolled my eyes. "Stop being gross."

He chuckled as I gave him a hug and a kiss goodbye. Rowan said his goodbye behind me and then followed me out the door. His hand kept brushing against mine as we walked the corridor to the elevator.

"Maybe we should take the stairs?" He nodded at them.

We were only three floors up, so I shrugged in agreement. He held the door open for a nurse to step out before we stepped in and made our way to the second floor, then the first. When we reached the landing, he pulled me aside, wrapped a hand behind my neck, and kissed me. His tongue delving into my mouth, branding me with the intensity of the kiss.

"I can't do this anymore," he breathed against me. "I can't be apart from you much longer." His hands were on my breasts over my blouse, mine were under the jacket of his suit, relishing how hard he felt beneath it all.

"We're in a hospital stairwell," I whispered. I wasn't even wearing a skirt today. He groaned against me.

"I'm coming over tonight."

"Rowan."

"Sprite." He looked into my eyes. "I'm coming over tonight."

"Okay."

MY BEDROOM DOOR opened sometime after I'd fallen asleep. I bolted upright in bed when I saw the large figure walk inside.

"It's just me."

"Rowan," I breathed out. "You can't just—how did you get in?"

"You gave me a key, remember?"

"Not to keep."

"Well, I kept it."

I smiled into the dark. "What time is it? I didn't think you were going to come."

"It's only ten." I heard rustling and knew he was undressing. The bed dipped a few beats after and I shivered as he scooted over to me, pressing his naked chest against my barely clothed body. His lips found mine in an unrushed kiss.

"I miss you so much, Sprite."

"I miss you," I whispered against his mouth.

"Let me stay."

I shook my head, my nose tapping against his. "You know I can't. Not until we know for sure she's out of our lives."

"I hate this."

"So do I."

He kissed me again, harder this time, with more desperation than the previous kiss held. I wrapped my legs around his waist and my arms around his neck as he pushed me onto my back and climbed over me. He pulled back for a moment, long enough to pull my T-shirt over my head and drag my underwear down my legs. His went next and then he was right over me again, kissing me deeply, his hands everywhere—on my breasts, my thighs, and my waist, which had me arching up to meet his erection, thick and ready between my legs. His fingers ran through my folds and into me, teasing, making me wet and ready and desperate for release. I ground against him, moaned out his name, tugged the ends of his hair, wishing I could make out his face. With no warning or hesitation, he thrust into me. I gasped loudly, my nails scraping down his back.

"Fuck," he breathed as he pressed his forehead against mine and drew out slowly. "Fuck, Tessa."

He brought his cheek against mine, the prickle of his light beard sending goose bumps down my flesh. He pressed open-mouthed kisses along my jaw, nipping and sucking his way to my earlobe as he fucked me deeper, harder, until I was panting his name and my nails were digging into his flesh so hard I was sure I'd draw blood. He pulled back slightly, bringing a hand up to my forehead, pushing my hair off of it. In the dark, I couldn't see his eyes, but I could make out his set jaw and long nose. I brought my hand up, pressing the tips of my fingers against his full lips. He parted them and sucked my fingertips into his mouth.

"I can feel how close you are," he said against my fingertips. "Gripping my cock so fucking tight."

I gripped again. On purpose that time, though my body was coiled with need and crumbling in pleasure I couldn't make up even if I wanted to. He bowed his head, his lips capturing mine again as I shattered around him and he inside me, my name a growl on his lips. He set his forehead against mine and breathed out as we caught our breaths.

"Happy birthday, Sprite."

I wrapped my arms around him again and pulled him close, wishing I never had to let go.

CHAPTER THIRTY-FOUR

TESSA

I MADE Rowan slink away in the middle of the night. He had another meeting with his attorney in the morning anyway and we were hoping it would be the last one. So, after much deliberation on his part, he gave me a kiss, snuck into Miles's room to give him a kiss, and left. Hours later when I crawled out of bed, I found myself standing in front of a very sad-looking Miles, who was sitting there just staring at his waffles.

"What's wrong?"

He brought his gaze to mine. "When is Rowan coming back?"

"What?" I set my mug down and gave him my full attention.

"When is he coming back? I miss him."

"Soon, babe. Very soon." I looked at his untouched plate. "Do you want more syrup?"

He shook his head. "Rowan puts whipped cream on them."

"I'll get you whipped cream then." I pulled it out of the fridge, stacked the waffles, and sprayed whipped cream on them. He moped some more. I sighed. "What?"

"He makes faces."

"Miles." I exhaled, setting the can down. "You're eating chocolate chip waffles. Most kids your age would kill to be eating this right now."

"I just miss him," he said in a small voice, his bottom lip quivering as he looked at me. My shoulders fell. I walked around the counter and over to him, pulling him into a hug.

"I miss him too."

"Is Rowan going to be my daddy?"

"You mean if he moves in?"

Miles nodded against me.

"Miles." I pulled back to look at his face. "Rowan is your daddy."

"My real daddy?"

"Yes. What do you think about that?"

"I like it." He smiled.

I cut up his waffles and followed his instructions on how Rowan prepared them for him—adding chocolate syrup and more whipped cream. I was surprised Rowan would allow this breakfast for Miles. It looked like something he wouldn't go near.

"So, I take it you like Rowan."

"I like him a lot." He stuffed an oversized bite into this mouth.

"Would you like to change your last name and be Miles Frederick Hawthorne?"

He glanced up, brows pulling in slightly. "What's Hawthorb?"

"Hawthorne. Ha-th-orne," I said. "It's Rowan's last name and since he's your daddy, it can be your last name as well."

His lips pursed as he seemingly mulled it over. Finally, he nodded. "I like it."

"Good."

"What's your last name?"

"Monte."

"Not Hawthorbe?"

"Hawthorne," I said. "And no."

"Why not?"

"Because Rowan and I aren't married."

"I'm not married."

I sighed heavily and explained the difference between marriage and being born into a name. Miles wasn't impressed.

"When is Uncle Freddie coming home?"

"This week." I smiled wide at that.

Freddie had a long way to go, but he was making progress. He'd start rehab four days a week, but at least they were letting him come home. Dad had been staying in Freddie's apartment and Mom in Celia's. My grandmother left for upstate earlier in the week. She'd wanted to plan a birthday party for me once Freddie was discharged, but I asked her to leave it alone. I wasn't sure how Freddie would feel about a three-hour drive right now and I wasn't really in the mood to celebrate anyway.

AT PRIM, I met with my team and went over the status on the furniture for the hotel. Everything seemed to be running smoothly until Ryan called me into his office to tell me Natasha and he got into a disagreement and she wouldn't sign the contract to provide the fabrics. I sat across from him and let him get the whole thing off his chest, trying my best not to reach over the desk to strangle him.

"All you had to do was smile, go over the papers with her, and have her sign them," I said. "Instead, you chased away what could potentially be our best fabric maker out there. And the cheapest. What the hell, Ryan?"

"She's a royal—"

"Don't you fucking dare." I glared at him. "If you're going to call her a bitch, you might as well go ahead and call yourself one, too, because you're acting like one."

He balked. "Is everyone on their period right now?"

"Oh, lovely." I scoffed. "Let's bring that into the equation."

"I don't understand," he said, lowering his voice. He truly looked clueless. "I told her the skirt she was wearing was nice and she went off on me."

"How did you say it?"

"I don't know." He shrugged. "Nice skirt."

"Like that? In that tone?" I was missing something. He sounded bored.

"I looked at it." He stood. "Stand up so I can show you." I did, waiting for him to continue. His eyes traveled the length of me slowly, provocatively, and then he sat, gave me another once-over, and in a low, husky voice said, "Nice skirt."

I blinked and slowly sat again. Had I not been stupid obsessing over Rowan and the way he made me feel when he looked at me, I would've totally been turned on. "You've got to be kidding," I said.

"No, and then she told me she had a serious boyfriend and that I should be ashamed of myself for objectifying women just because they're wearing a form-fitting skirt," he said, throwing his hands up. "What the fuck?"

"Maybe avoid commenting on a woman's wardrobe, especially if you're going to do it like you want to bend her over your desk."

His eyes widened slightly. "I didn't mean to imply that."

"But you did."

"Jesus Christ. I have never in the thirty-four years of my life had a woman get offended over something like that," he said. "I have three sisters! I would never—"

"I'll talk to Natasha and fix this," I said as I stood. "Hopefully. I'll keep you posted. If not, we'll use the blues from Hawthorne. They're providing us with the rest of the colors."

Ryan smiled. "What's going on with Hawthorne?"

"None of your business." I walked over to the door.

"I heard you may be moving in together soon."

"What?" I whipped around to face him. "He said that?"

"Where else would I get that sort of information?"

"I swear, men gossip more than women do," I muttered, walking out of his office.

"Please send Natasha flowers on my behalf," he shouted.

"I'm not your secretary," I shouted back.

"Ask Chloe to."

"I'm not your secretary either," Chloe shouted back.

I headed to the fifth floor, inhaling the woodsy scent. Sam wasn't in his usual workspace, so I walked right up to Rowan's door and knocked once, twice, until he invited me to come inside.

HE WAS SITTING behind his desk, sleeves rolled up, exposing his muscular forearms as he signed a paper. When he looked up at me, a smile that warmed me all over lit up his expression.

"Hey, baby."

"Hey." I smiled, closing the door behind me and making my

way around his desk. He pushed his chair away, pulled me on top of his legs, and cupped my face to give me an unrushed, soft kiss that had my pulse skyrocketing by the time I pulled back.

"How was Miles this morning?"

"Sad." I adjusted my position and wrapped my arms around his neck, resting my head on his chest.

"Why sad?" His hand ran a comforting line down the length of my spine.

"He wants Rowan to make his waffles, Rowan to do this, Rowan to do that," I said. "He misses his daddy."

Rowan grinned. "He said that?"

"He did."

"He called me his dad?"

"He did." I couldn't help my own smile.

"You told him?" He urged me to sit up so he could see my face and I obliged, grinning as I did so.

"Really?"

I nodded before he put both hands on my face and pulled me into another kiss. "We're going out to celebrate."

I laughed. "Where? It's a school night."

He reached over me and clicked his mouse, opening his calendar. I glanced at it with him. All his meetings seemed to be on there. Today's date had two things: Email Enrique and meeting with Sprite. My gaze slid to his.

"Meeting with Sprite? Seriously, Rowan?" I shook my head. "That doesn't sound professional."

He kissed my shoulder. "Who cares? I'm the only one who looks at this."

"You need a secretary," I said, looking at all of the meetings. How did he keep track of these?

"I have one. Rosa's on maternity leave. She comes back in a few weeks."

"You couldn't get a temp in the meantime?"

"Not like Rosa. I don't trust anyone else around my stuff." His eyes twinkled. "Unless you're available."

I laughed outright. "You can't afford me."

"Probably not." He chuckled and leaned against the back of the chair. I stood, grabbed my sketchbook, and sat at the table that was on the far side of his office. "Why don't you just sketch directly on the tablet?"

I made a face. "I hate technology for stuff like that."

"Seriously?" He joined me, seeming to take up all of my space. "You don't have a tablet you sketch in?"

"Yeah, but I'd rather do the first few drafts on paper. I feel like I find more mistakes when I can't erase them. It's weird."

He made me sketch on the tablet anyway and I did only because no one had used it before and I could see he was dying for someone to try it.

"You're so good," he said with a sense of awe in his voice that made my cheeks warm.

As I sketched, I told him about the Ryan thing, adding, "So, yeah, you should probably talk to your friend."

"Fucking Ryan."

"I know."

"We were so fucking close," he said. "I need to buy that company."

I stopped sketching. "You're joking."

"Of course, I'm not. How much money could she possibly want? I've seen their factory," he said. "Natasha's, Ana in Guatemala, Blanca in Nicaragua. They must have a price."

"Why not buy big shipments from them?" I asked. "Help them grow their companies instead of going in there like a damn invading army and taking over."

He stayed quiet for a long moment. When I realized he wasn't going to say anything else, I went back to the sketches. I made a few designs. One with tiny spaceships, another with small wolves, a third with owls.

"I can keep going," I said, setting the pencil down. "But you get the idea. Do you have any ideas for the logo?"

"Fairy wings."

"Be serious." I laughed, slapping his arm playfully. He caught my hand.

"I am serious."

"You know you can't call it Sprite, right? That's taken by a pretty big company."

"Really?" He lifted my hand to his mouth and bit it lightly. "I wasn't aware."

"When are you going to tell me about what happened with the lawyer?"

"Everything's done and being processed." His eyes hadn't stopped glimmering with happiness since I got there, which in turn made me happy.

"Do you want to come with me to pick up Miles?"

"Hell yes."

When we got there and Miles spotted us, he took off in a run, opening his arms wide. Rowan crouched and caught him in a hug, enveloping him in his arms. I waved at the teacher as we started to walk away. Rowan hadn't let go of Miles.

"I've missed you so much," he said into his hair. Miles pulled back long enough for me to give him a kiss. He looked at Rowan.

"I thought you left because I made you mad."

"What? No way," Rowan said. "Nothing you do could make me angry enough to ever leave you. I just wanted to keep you safe while I took care of some things."

"From the lady at school?"

Rowan stayed quiet for a beat, looking over at me. I shrugged. "That was part of it, but now I can come hang out with you whenever you want."

"Are you going to move in?"

Rowan chuckled. "We'll have to see what your mom says."

"Mommy doesn't make waffles like you, or dinner."

"Be gentle with Mommy. She has a lot on her plate," Rowan said, wrapping an arm around my shoulder as we walked. I'd never felt so happy in my life than I was in that moment.

CHAPTER THIRTY-FIVE

TESSA

ROWAN WASN'T KIDDING when he'd said these galas were stuffy and obnoxious. They were necessary though. I figured that out after the second conversation I had with a woman about the curtains in her house and how she couldn't find the right fabric for them. Rowan's attention was on me the entire time. Even as we spoke to different groups of people, he let me know he was right there, his fingers brushing against mine, his gaze catching mine briefly. He was wearing a tuxedo that I'd been dying to rip off him since the moment he put it on.

"You okay?" Rowan asked as he pulled me away from the bankers we'd been talking to.

"I'm fine." I smiled, linking my fingers through his. "Do you think I didn't go to events like this in Paris?"

"I don't want to think about you in Paris at all." He leaned down and kissed my jaw, his breath tickling my neck. "The only thing I've thought about all night is tearing that dress off you."

"Hm. We're having the same thoughts then."

He pulled back, his eyes smoldering. "Really?"

"Yes, really."

"Have you given my proposal any thought?"

"You haven't proposed," I said, arching an eyebrow.

"I seem to remember many proposals." He mimicked my expression. I felt a blush creep up on my neck and face.

"The shower doesn't count. Nor the bed."

"Hm." He made a little growly sound at the back of his throat that threatened to make me cave right on the spot. He pulled me away from the people beside us and pushed me against the column, leaning into me and sucking on my exposed neck. My breath hitched.

"What about the kitchen counter? Does that count?"

"Nuh-uh." I tried to shake my head, but I could barely breathe.

"Against your office window?" he rasped against me. "On my balcony? In the elevator?"

"Rowan." My voice was a pant as need built between my legs.

The proposals were all tests to see if I'd say yes when he really asked me. I knew that. Of course, I'd said no every single time, even in the throes of passion, which drove him absolutely crazy. The butterflies in my stomach lit up at the thought of just how crazy. His divorce was officially finalized, but I liked the pace in which things had been moving. I didn't want to ruin it with a proposal. Truth was, I was pretty sure I was scaring him by saying no.

"Well, isn't this a picture."

I closed my eyes as Rowan pulled away from me and we faced Camryn. Of course, she'd be there.

"What do you want?" Rowan asked.

Camryn smiled as she looked at me. "I heard the kid is yours after all."

I was glad we were standing behind a column and out of sight from the crowd, because I felt my blood drain and then shoot back into me with fierceness. I let go of Rowan's hand and took a step toward her. Whatever she saw on my face made her take a step back, directly into the marble column. Her eyes widened.

"You know, your pathetic, sorry existence never bothered me," I seethed, adrenaline rushing through my veins. "But if you come anywhere near my son again, I will fucking kill you." I must have lifted my hand and gripped her throat in my rage, because when Rowan grabbed me by the shoulders, that was where it was.

Camryn panted, grabbing her neck with both hands. "She's attacking me!"

"I don't know what you're talking about," Rowan said. "I suggest you take her advice and leave us the fuck alone."

I was shaking as Rowan escorted me out of the gala and into the first taxi we found. When we got to his house, he helped me out, making sure the short train of my dress didn't get caught in anything, and when we got inside, he pushed me against the door.

"You're so fucking hot," he said, his lips crashing against mine. His tongue swept into my mouth in one swift motion, rattling my pulse. I pulled his jacket off, the vest under it, tugged at his pants. He tore at my dress, ripping the zipper as he tried to tug it down. When it pooled at my feet, he took a step back, his gaze smoldering as he dragged it over every inch of my naked body.

"You weren't wearing any underwear?"

I smiled, shaking my head a split second before his body was pressed against mine again. He devoured my mouth as his hands touched every inch of my skin and dipped between my legs, spreading them slightly. I complied, letting him slip his fingers through my folds, arching my back off the door when he pushed his fingers inside me. I gasped, grappling for his dress shirt, the waistband of his pants. I needed it off. I needed him inside me. He let out a low chuckle when I pleaded for this, his eyes on mine, his nose just inches from mine.

"Please," I said again.

"I love you," he said against my lips, his other hand working on his pants as he continued to push his fingers in and out of me, making me wetter and wetter with each motion.

"I love you, now please," I whined.

"Marry me."

"Rowan, shut upppppppp." The desperate cry ripped from the back of my throat.

"Marry me."

"Ask me again tomorrow," I panted. He took his fingers out of me, and I whined again. "What the—"

His hands grabbed my ass, hauling me up against the door as he thrust into me hard. Shit. My head fell back with a loud *thump*.

"Oh my god," I said again and again until I climaxed around him and he pulsed deep and hard inside me.

He exhaled heavily, dropping his forehead onto my shoulder, still holding me up. "You are the most badass woman I know."

I laughed, unfolding my legs from his waist and finding my footing again. "You ripped my dress."

"You can sew it back together." He winked as he picked up

the rest of our discarded clothes. "Maybe you can start sketching your wedding dress."

I laughed. "Probably not."

It was a lie. I'd sketched more than just one wedding dress in the last couple of months, but he didn't need to know that just yet.

CHAPTER THIRTY-SIX

TESSA

I DECIDED that if there would ever be a time to do something about Camryn, it was then, and it was with that thought in mind that I called Mildred. She answered after a few rings and I held my breath for a beat before saying, "Mildred, it's Tessa."

I'd rehearsed my speech a million times and it sounded dumber each time I recited it, so I squeezed my eyes shut and hoped for the best. I was sitting in the most incredible office in Manhattan, an office that rivaled rich men in Wall Street. I was damn good at my job. I was also a damn good mother, sister, daughter, and girlfriend. There was nothing Mildred could say that would take away from any of my accomplishments. Those were the things I reminded myself of.

"Tessa?" I could hear the confusion in her voice. "Is everything all right? How are your parents? Freddie? I heard he was in an accident."

"They're fine. Everyone's fine. I'm calling about Rowan."

"Oh. What about him?" Her sudden icy tone gave me pause.

"You aren't aware of this because he hasn't spoken to you," I started, "but he has a son. With me. And I know you're Camryn's number one supporter, but I figured I'd call you and let you know that she isn't allowed anywhere near my son, and neither is anyone who wishes me, him, or Rowan any harm."

"I . . . a son?" she whispered. "How . . . when . . . how old is he?"

"He'll be four soon."

"A four-year-old son, and I'm only just now hearing about this?" she asked, her voice growing louder.

"Like I said, I don't want him near anyone who wishes any of us harm."

"I've never wished you harm."

"No, you just wished I'd go away so that your son could be with the evil bitch he married."

"It was the right thing for him to do," she said. "Camryn understood what was expected of her."

"Camryn is a disgusting human being who's put Rowan through the wringer with this divorce. She also showed up at my son's daycare and scared the daylights out of him. This is a courtesy call. If you can't meet me halfway, I'm going to assume you want nothing to do with your grandson. For the record, I don't care one way or another. As far as I'm concerned, he has more than enough love in his life."

"Does Alistair know?"

I rolled my eyes just as Chloe walked into my office with a folder in her hand and a huge smile on her face.

Medellin Fabrics signed, she mouthed with a thumbs-up. My smile was wide as I returned her thumbs-up enthusiastically.

"Alistair knows."

"He told his father?" Mildred whispered.

"From what I understand, you had a choice—your son or Camryn, and you chose wrong. It was nice catching up. I have to go. I have a lot of work to get done today."

I hung up before she could get another word in.

Later that night, when Rowan came over, I told him what I did. He stared at me blankly from across the kitchen island.

"How did you get her phone number?"

"Sam."

He shook his head, still gaping. "Of course. Well, what did she say?"

"I hung up on her."

"You hung up on my mother?"

I shrugged. "It was an impulsive move, I know."

"That's one way of putting it." He chuckled. "That would explain the five phone calls I received and ignored from her today. I haven't listened to the voice messages she left, but I can only assume they're going to be very interesting." He reached over and put his hand over mine. "Camryn called today."

I took my hand from under his on instinct. "And?"

"And she apologized. She also said she hoped I was happy with my 'crazy ass girlfriend,'" he air quoted. The way he said it made me laugh.

"That doesn't sound like much of an insult coming from her."

He scoffed. "There's crazy and then there's Camryn."

"Right." We stayed quiet for a moment before I asked, "Do you think she'll leave us alone?"

"Yes. I really do. She also told me to apologize to you on her behalf."

"That I don't believe."

"Why would I lie?" He walked around the island, stood behind me, and wrapped his arms around me, tucking his face into the crook of my neck.

"I filed a petition for a name change," I said, "for Miles."

Rowan pulled back, turned my chair to face him, and searched my eyes. "Really?"

"Really." I smiled, bringing my hand up to tickle his beard. "He should have his dad's name, don't you think? Keep the Hawthorne family name going and all that."

His eyes blurred with unshed tears as he nodded. "Thank you." He wrapped his arms around me again, crushing me to him. "Thank you for this."

CHAPTER THIRTY-SEVEN

TESSA

"LET'S GO ON THE CANOE," Rowan said into my ear after lunch.

I looked over at Miles, who was lying on the couch with Freddie. He was tracing the scar on my brother's face, looking at him in awe for having survived that attack. He still hadn't given us the details. Not that I'd expected him to. I was just happy he was with us.

We'd all gone to my grandmother's cottage for the weekend and Rowan was the only one who'd been on a canoe. He had been rowing back home on his machine, but it wasn't the same.

He explained exactly how countless times while I sat on my yoga mat staring at him as he rowed. It made me hot every time. Even the way his sweat trickled down his face was hot. The way his lips formed an O during his pull was hot. The way his back, legs, and stomach tightened with each motion.

"I'll go if you take off your shirt," I said.

He grinned. "I'll take off more than just my shirt."

"TMI," Freddie said from the couch. "We can hear you."

Miles sat up and glanced over. "Why would you take off all your clothes?"

"Because Daddy's weird," I said.

Rowan chuckled, slapping my ass.

"What does motherfucker mean?" Miles asked, and my wide eyes shot in my son's direction.

Freddie cough-laughed. "Where'd you hear that?"

"Daddy."

"Rowan," I shot him a stern look, slapping his stomach.

"You act like I called him that word." Rowan rolled his eyes. He looked at Miles. "That's a bad word, buddy. We don't say that."

"You say it."

"Yeah, but I'm an adult."

"So?"

"Adults are dumb sometimes. You can't repeat everything we say."

Miles shrugged, a little nonchalant lift a shoulder, and looked at Freddie again. "Can we watch *Minions*?"

"Again?"

"Yes."

"Hey," Rowan said. "What happens at the end of *Frozen*?"

Freddie frowned deeply as he sat up. "How the eff am I supposed to know? You watch *Frozen*?"

"I have a four-year-old. I've watched it. I keep falling asleep before it ends. Do Anna and Hans get married?"

"Not every Disney movie ends in marriage," I said.

"Princess ones do," Rowan argued.

"Not all of them. Hello, *Moana?*"

He shrugged, pulling my hand. "Let's go."

I let him lead me outside and I waved at my parents and grandmother who were gardening. It was Mom and Grandma Joan's favorite past time, and somehow Dad got dragged into it every time. Rowan went up to them, plucked a rose, and jogged back over to me.

"Seriously, Rowan?" Mom called out. "I was about to plant it."

"I'll get you another one tomorrow," he called back. "I need to impress my girlfriend."

They laughed in unison. I shook my head, smiling as he handed me the rose. When we got to the canoe, I noted the little cushions with the tablecloth spread between them.

"We just ate," I said.

"Can you just sit and enjoy this?"

"Okay," I said. "Do I get the paddles?"

He shot me a glare. I put my hands up and let him row us away from the shore. He stopped in the middle, one of our usual spots, and exhaled.

"It's a nice day."

"It is," I agreed, looking around. I stopped when I saw a new cottage. "That's new."

"It's cute," he commented.

"You should sell your apartment and get one so you can be closer to the water," I suggested. "You'd be less grumpy."

"I'm not grumpy."

"Sometimes." I fought a smile. He reached under the white

tablecloth and pulled out a bottle of wine and two glasses. I raised an eyebrow. "Color me impressed."

He chuckled. "Good." He set them aside. I waited, but he didn't move to serve it, so I closed my eyes and tilted my face toward the sun, breathing it all in. Long seconds passed before he said, "You are so beautiful."

I slowly opened my eyes at his tone, which was rough and gravely and full of heat. Rowan leaned forward, placing both hands on my knees, spreading them apart so he could settle between them, and then he put his forehead against mine and breathed out. I did the same, holding his hands on my lap.

"Have I told you that you're the best thing that's ever happened to me?" he whispered.

I nodded against him. "All the time."

"Have I told you that I think about you obsessively?"

I laughed lightly. "No, that's creepy."

"I'm a creep then, because you're all I think about. Aside from Miles, but that goes without saying."

"I think about you creepily, obsessively too," I admitted.

"Yeah?"

"Yeah."

"I think I was thirteen when you bewitched me." He pulled back slightly, his eyes searching mine. "You looked at me one of those Saturdays when I was visiting Monte and I thought you had to be the prettiest girl in the world." He paused, his thumbs brushing against the backs of my hands. "I've traveled a lot since then and I have to say, I was definitely right about that."

I felt tears brim in my eyes. I tried to blink them back, but they trickled down my cheeks lightly. Ro brought a hand up and brushed them away.

"I never believed in marriage," he said. "Ultimately, it's just a stupid piece of paper, but I really, really want to sign that stupid piece of paper with your name beside mine. When our kids grow up, I want to be able to look at them and say, 'You see that woman over there? She has some serious magic and somehow, I was the one who caught it all.'" His Adam's apple bobbed. "What I'm trying to say is that I love you, Tessa Monte. I bleed for you. You're the only woman in the world who can make me believe that love exists. The only woman in the world I'd ever want tied to me for an eternity. The only woman I could ever envision raising my children. Please marry me."

"I bleed for you too," I whispered, emotion clogging my throat. "Yes. I'll marry you."

He reached under the tablecloth and brought out a small box before opening it to show me the most beautiful diamond I'd ever seen. His eyes held mine as he took it out and slipped it onto my finger. "I promise I'll be the best husband I can. I promise to listen to you and help carry your burdens. I can't promise that I'll cook for you every night or rub your feet after a long day every night, but I promise that I'll try. Above anything, I promise that I'll always talk to you, always respect you, and always put you above everything, even my work, even myself."

I couldn't even speak. I looked down at my shaky hand and the ring on it, and threw my arms around him, rocking the canoe back and forth. The wine rolled. When I finally sat in my side of the canoe, he grinned and nodded toward the shore, to the house I had pointed out earlier. "You see that little cottage they're building?" He pointed at a house not much bigger than my grandmother's. It was white with a lot of windows.

"Yeah."

"It's ours. They should be finished building next month."

I pulled back. "Are you serious?"

"Dead serious," he said. "I tried to buy your old house, but Sam talked me out of it. He said we needed new memories and I agree. This cottage will be a blank slate. New cottage, new family, new beginnings." He kissed the tip of my nose and pulled away. "But the sculls stay. I can't get rid of those."

I laughed. "I wouldn't dream of asking you to. I can't believe you built us a house here."

"Miles needs a place to see the stars," he said, bringing his thumb up to my lower lip. "And we need a place to escape from the world."

I kissed him then, not because of the cottage and not because of the ring, but because of everything he was and everything he'd be.

"You really do love me," I said, smiling.

"I don't just love you, Sprite. I bleed for you. Only for you."

EPILOGUE

ROWAN

"DAD, JUST LET THEM PLAY," I said for the fourth time in a row.

Dad, Mariah, and Harrison had come to the cottage for the day, and my dad just couldn't let the kid run around like a normal twelve-year-old. He kept worrying he'd get hurt.

"He will get hurt," I said. "You know that, right?"

Dad sighed heavily. "I'm too old for this."

I laughed. "As someone who grew up with you as my father, I'm going to have to disagree. You seem to be the perfect age for this."

He really was. He was attentive with both Mariah and Harrison. Samson and I still thought it was a little weird that we had a twelve-year-old brother, but we loved him and treated him like he was one of us, because he was. Mom was still living in London, but she visited once in a while. She said she didn't want her grandkids not to know her. The environment seemed to quiet down when she was around, though, despite the fact that she'd remarried and seemed extremely happy with Harold.

I watched Mom as she talked to Tessa, who was holding our

one-year-old daughter, Luna, in her arms. The moment Mom glanced away, Tessa's eyes found mine and widened.

Get me out of here, she mouthed.

I chuckled. It wasn't that Tessa and my mom didn't get along, it was that they didn't agree on anything, but Mom loved Tessa. She'd said as much at our wedding. She also said she didn't remember saying such horrible things to her in the past. She said it was too long ago and her memory was awful, but she admitted that she'd been wrong. We didn't care. Camryn's name was never brought up—ever. I didn't know how she was doing and didn't care. The only people who mattered to me were Miles, Luna, and Tessa. They were my world. Everything else could wait. My brother jogged over with a beer in each hand and handed one to me.

"Freddie's here," he said. "Which means these will be gone in ten minutes."

I chuckled, taking a sip. "He said he stopped drinking because it was giving him a beer gut and he needed to have abs by June."

"Well, it's July," Sam said, raising an eyebrow. "And here we are."

"Fuck you." I scowled. "My abs are fine."

Sam laughed, taking a sip of his beer. "So, what's going on? Is Tessa going to leave Prim and come work with us full time?"

"I think so." I exhaled.

I fucking hoped so. After our socks launched three years ago, we'd expanded RHS Designs and added winter hats and then gloves. I wanted to add a children's clothing line to bring Tessa's Mommy and Me and Daddy and Me idea to fruition. Problem was that she liked Prim. The sky-rise and the pay and the demand. We worked together pretty often anyway, this would just mean we'd work together ninety percent of the time instead of just fifty.

"I'll have to keep trying to convince her," I said. "We're finally done remodeling the house. That was step one. If she does come on board for this, I would want to open a boutique to sell everything in. Nothing big."

"That can work." Sam nodded. "She'd like that."

"I think so."

"Chloe would probably want to leave with her," he added. "Tessa was trying to get her promoted, but she seems to like working side by side with her."

I smiled. "Well, in that case, we'd have to make room for her."

"What in the world are you looking at?" he asked, looking at my phone. I pushed the side button quickly.

"Nothing."

Samson chuckled loudly. "Tessa!"

She glanced up, shot daggers at me, and then smiled at my brother for rescuing her from the conversation with my mom. She shifted Luna into my mom's arms and headed our way.

"Thanks for nothing," she said to me and then looked at Sam. "What's up?"

"I think Rowan has a problem."

"What?"

"He's obsessed with mommy boards."

Tessa's eyes glimmered in amusement. She already knew this. We talked about it all the time because one freaking time we got into an argument, and I'd used the mommy board as my source of relief for teething.

"Don't start," I said before she could say anything and of course, that only made her laugh and look at my brother, who was also laughing.

"I keep telling him Luna's fine. He's worried that she isn't speaking enough," she said. "Guess why? Because the moms—"

"What moms?" Freddie asked, joining us. "By the way, Celia's on her way with Ben."

"You're kidding." Tessa's eyes widened. "She has so much explaining to do."

Freddie nodded and then looked at me. "What are you talking about?"

"Nothing."

"Oh, you know, Ro and his obsession with mommy boards," Sam said.

Tessa held her stomach as she laughed. If it weren't for the fact that the sound was one of my favorite things in the world and seeing her eyes light up made me feel warm all over, I would have been upset. Since it was and they did, I spent the rest of the afternoon fending off their stupid jokes. When everyone was gone and the kids were both sleeping peacefully in their rooms, I found her standing by the window that overlooked the lake. I walked up, wrapped my arms around her, and took a deep breath. Every morning, I asked myself how I had gotten as lucky as I had, and every morning I was left without an answer. Every night, I thanked the stars for bringing her into my life on more than one occasion.

"I love you, Sprite."

She glanced up at me. "I love you. Always."

AFTERWORD

Thank you SO much for reading!
Click here for a bonus scene from Rowan and Tessa: Extra scene from MWBTY

ALSO BY CLAIRE CONTRERAS

Also in Kindle Unlimited:

Kaleidoscope Hearts - brother's best friend romance

Paper Hearts - ultimate second-chance romance

Elastic Hearts - forbidden second-chance romance

Complete Hearts Series - all three bundled up in one

Prefer a standalone?

The Player - sports romance (Kindle Unlimited)

The Wilde One - music industry romance (Kindle Unlimited)

Want a little suspense with your romance?

There is No Light in Darkness - a little mystery, a lot of love.